T0328749

FENDING OFF THE WAR PARTY

Chance had fired fast and hard as the raiding party attacked. He did a fast job of emptying the Spencer rifle into the riders, killing two comancheros and wounding several Apaches, he thought. In another pass he had emptied a spare Henry rifle that Ike handed him. It was when they made their third pass at them—when Manuel killed the Indian pony—that Chance suddenly remembered what it was that marked the Apache as being different from the Comanche. And it almost cost him his life.

Books by Jim Miller

South of the Border
The Stranger from Nowhere
Carston's Law
Shootout in Sendero
Stagecoach to Fort Dodge
The 600 Mile Stretch
Rangers Reunited
Too Many Drifters
Hell with the Hide Off
The Long Rope
Rangers' Revenge

Published by POCKET BOOKS

THE EX-RANGERS

SOUTH OF THE BORDER

JIM MILLER

POCKET BOOKS
New York London Toronto Sydney Singapore

This book is a work of fiction. Names, characters, places and incidents are products of the author's imagination or are used fictitiously. Any resemblance to actual events or locales or persons, living or dead, is entirely coincidental.

An *Original* Publication of POCKET BOOKS

POCKET BOOKS, a division of Simon & Schuster, Inc.
1230 Avenue of the Americas, New York, NY 10020

ISBN: 978-1-5011-0994-2

First Pocket Books printing October 1993

11 10 9 8 7 6 5 4 3 2

Front cover illustration by Dennis Cook

Printed in the U.S.A

This one's for my youngest son, Michael,
just for being.

SOUTH OF THE BORDER

CHAPTER

★ 1 ★

Manuel couldn't get over how big the *norteamericano* was, especially sitting in the saddle the way he did. Without a doubt he would be very tall when he dismounted, but just sitting there with a sneer about his face, he still seemed bigger than most. And many of the *norteamericanos* were big, to be sure. But even more scary than the *norteamericano* was the look of fear on Rosa's face as she stood before him in front of their adobe hut. Standing beside her was her husband, José, a fearless man if ever there was one.

Manuel saw all of this from his place of hiding behind the barn. He feared for his sister's life, for Rosa was the only living relative he had left now and he loved her just as much as José did. He had, in fact, been working the small field when he saw the *norteamericano* and his *compañeros* ride up. As effortlessly as if he were a Gila monster moving about the desert, changing colors with the ease of nature, Manuel had made his way to the back of the barn, not forty feet from José's adobe structure. But he could not recall where the extra rifle was located in the barn, nor was he sure he could use it if he could find it. Manuel had never had the courage of his brother-in-law and Rosa and José knew it as well as he did. Still, that didn't seem to stop José Quesada from speaking his mind now, even to a well-armed man like the *norteamericano.*

"No, señor, I do not have the food you demand," he said with a look as proud as the tone of his voice. He was of medium height, in his fifties, his hair graying, his face wrinkled from years of hard work on this small parcel of land he called his own. He knew that the three mounted men before him were an odd mixture at best—a renegade Apache, probably a Lipan, a scraggly-looking comanchero, and the *norteamericano,* who did the talking for all of them. But José had talked with and fought all three of these breeds and managed to survive all of them over the years and he wouldn't quit now. "I have a wife and my children to consider first. No, sir, I do not have the food you demand. Nor would I give it to you if I did."

"So much for being polite," the big man, the *norteamericano,* said as he dismounted. The man took on a certain gruffness as a frown crossed his face now. If it was meant to scare José, it did not. The Mexican glared back at the man with as much defiance as he could muster, small as he was compared to his opponent.

The *norteamericano* struck him hard across the mouth, knocking him forcefully back against the adobe wall of his house, his *casa*. Before José could regain his balance, the big man had grabbed him by the shirtfront, pulled José to him, and punched him hard twice more. José was nearing unconsciousness and could barely see the children as they attacked the *norteamericano*. The big man easily pushed them away as he dropped José to the ground.

"Keep the little bastards away from me or I'll kill 'em next time, hear?" he said with a snarl, addressing Rosa, who quickly had her two children, a boy and a girl, encircled in her arms for protection.

"Let 'em be, Marcus," the comanchero said with what he must have considered to be a smile. His head was covered by a red bandana, topped off with a stovepipe hat with several bullet holes airing it out. His smile could have been permanent. The scar that ran from the edge of his mouth to just below his ear made it hard to tell when he was smiling and when he wasn't. Aside from his physical composition, all Rosa noticed at the moment was that he was much more soft-spoken than the man who had just beaten her husband. "Let's just git their food and git the hell outta here."

"Sí," Rosa said immediately. "Yes, take the food. It is in the kitchen. Take it all. But leave us alone. Please."

There was a pleading sound in her last words, a sound that struck the chord Monroe Marcus had been looking for in the old man. One way or another, he had put the fear of God into them, made them realize that he had come for food and it was food he aimed to get.

The comanchero dismounted and took the children inside with him, using them more as guides to locate the food than anything else, although he was sure the woman outside knew he would kill them in the blink of an eye if she tried anything funny.

"Got it all, Parsons?" Monroe Marcus demanded when he came out, his arms loaded with supplies.

"Don't it look like it?" the man named Parsons replied with a wicked grin. He wasn't about to tell Marcus that he hadn't taken it all, had left a smidgen of food for these good folks to exist on until they could provide some more game or find the nearest town and get more provisions. He stuffed the saddlebags of all three with the supplies and mounted his own horse.

Rosa noticed that throughout the whole incident the Indian had remained stoic and silent.

José was just coming to as the renegades rode off with most of his food. It wasn't until the outlaws were out of sight that Manuel ran toward them from the barn, a look of concern about him as he asked how they were. The whole family, including the children, must have known he was in the barn, watching the whole thing, for all they did was give him a degrading look.

Inside, Rosa did her best to repair José's wounds, the worst of which seemed to be some bruised or cracked ribs.

"Where were you, Manuel?" Rosa finally asked with a deep frown. "When we need your help you are nowhere around."

Manuel could only shrug. "I crept up to the barn, but could not remember where the rifle was. Besides, if I had fired, I might have injured one of you instead."

Rosa gave her brother a hard glare as she scooped up her medicinals and padded out of the room, her disgust obvious.

"Don't be so hard on the man," a more sympathetic

José said to his wife. "He is right, we might have been hit. Or worse yet, killed by that *pistolero.*"

"I'm sorry, José," Manuel said in a humble manner. "I should have done more. I should have done better. Please forgive me."

José waved a hand at the man, as though to dismiss his words. "Forgiveness is for the man of the cloth," he said. "If you want forgiveness, forgive yourself for now." When it didn't seem as though his words had done any good, José placed a firm hand on his brother-in-law's arm, gave him a steadfast look, and said, "Manuel, I want you to get our best horse saddled and ready to ride."

Manuel was perplexed by the man's words. "But, José, you cannot ride in your condition."

"No, but you can. I have a mission for you, Manuel. And I guarantee you that if you accomplish it, all the saints in all their heavens will forgive you for an eternity to come."

"Really?" Manuel said in astonishment.

José nodded his head slowly, surely, seriously. "Really."

CHAPTER

Jeremiah Younger was a bit of an oddity. He seemed to be long in everything. Not big, just long. Even in his seated position at the card table in the rear of Ernie Johnson's Saloon it was evident he was a gangly sort. Long arms and long legs. But what Ernie kept an eye on with this sort was those long bony fingers the man had. To some they might seem merely slender, but to Ernie, who owned the saloon, they were a sign of dexterity, a sign that the man they belonged to could well be a card sharp with more than a few tricks up his sleeve.

If Ernie Johnson was sure of anything, it was that this Jeremiah Younger was a descendent of some kind of river-rat gambler. He was decked out in what seemed to be the attire of those who made their living at dealing cards. His coat was apparently custom made—it had to be for someone his size—of the finest broadcloth. His trousers were made of fine material also. The shirt was likely one of those fancy types that came with French ruffles, although Ernie wasn't sure. All he knew was that it was a sight more expensive than the plain white shirts he was used to wearing. But for all his fancy looks, he didn't seem to be drawing much of a crowd. Or maybe it was because it was just past midafternoon and most of the workingmen were out there working rather than wasting their time on the foolishness this man could hand out.

When Younger signaled for a beer, Ernie took his own sweet time getting it to him. "How much longer did you plan on staying around, Mr. Younger?" he asked as he placed the beer on the gaming table.

Jeremiah Younger just smiled. "If there is one thing I have, my good man, it is patience," he said as he took a sip of the half-warm beer.

"Oh?"

"Why certainly. There must be a payday in this town sometime. And I've enough funds to defray my expenses for quite some time to come. Surely you don't mind my taking up space at your table, do you?" he added when he saw a slight frown on Ernie's face.

The proprietor raised a cautious eyebrow. "Long as you don't drive away the business."

"I understand completely," was all Ernie heard the gambler say as he walked back to the bar. Something in his mind told him the man was smiling as he spoke.

Chance Carston made his way through the batwing doors a few minutes later. Doffing his Stetson, he slapped the dust off on his denims, wiped his forearm across his brow, and brought away a sleeve filled with sweat. "Summer ain't quite over, Ernie," he said with a half smile.

"Tell me about it," the bartender replied.

"If you've got anything close to tasting cold, I'll take it, hoss," Chance said, and Ernie drew him a beer. His beer was half gone when Chance noticed that there was hardly anyone in the saloon, thinking that even the deadbeats had found someplace cooler to spend their afternoons.

"Well, now, a man of leisure, are you?" he heard Younger say behind him. "Perhaps you'd care to while away the afternoon with a game of chance, eh?"

It could be said that Chance Carston had the curiosity of a cat. Of course, there were those—to include his father and brother—who laid claim to Chance having the luck of a cat with nine lives. "Oh? And just what kind of a flimflam are you pulling, mister?" Chance said as he approached the gaming table, pulled out a wooden chair, turned it backward, and seated himself. He placed his beer on the table before him.

"Well, sir, there are always the pasteboards," Younger said with his ever-present smile, tapping an idle finger on a deck of cards off to his side.

Chance shook his head. "Ain't enough here to get a good game of poker going."

"Then there is always my favorite," the gambler said as he dug down in a pocket and pulled out three thimbles and a lone pea-shaped object. "A dollar a try. Keep your eye on the pea now." In a deft manner, Jeremiah Younger maneuvered the thimbles around before him. "Now, then, where's the pea?" he said when he was through.

Chance pointed toward the thimble in the center

and Younger, with a half-clenched fist, lifted the thimble to reveal it empty of any pea. He was about to tell Chance that he owed him a dollar when he felt Chance's big hand slam down on his own hand, holding it in place. The force of the blow sent the remaining two thimbles rolling across the table, each of them as empty as the center thimble. When Chance dug a finger into the center of Jeremiah Younger's wrist, the lone pea came tumbling out, rolling a ways on the table before it stopped.

"Thimblerig, you're in the wrong profession," Chance growled at the man, his grip still firmly in place over the gambler's slender hand. "River rats like you followed our camps all through the war, trying to take our money."

"But—"

"You pull that trick on me again and I swear them skinny things you call fingers will never be of any use to you at a table like this again in your lifetime."

Chance never had been much on words, as far as preaching right and wrong to a person, but he was getting the sudden urge to be so with this so-called gambler. He was on his feet and about to lay down the law to Jeremiah Younger when the batwing doors abruptly pushed open, spoiling the moment for him.

The man in the saloon entrance was short, wearing a wide sombrero, indicating he was likely from south of the border somewhere. *"¿Es esto Twin Rifles?"* he asked in a hoarse voice.

"That's a fact, friend," Ernie Johnson said. "You look like you need a drink." That was Ernie, always selling the product.

"¿Dónde está Señor Carston?" he said next, ignoring the bartender and his offer of some liquid.

Chance frowned before saying, "One of 'em's right here."

Which is when the stranger in the doorway fell to the floor unconscious.

"Well, I'll be damned," Chance all but whispered as he rolled the man over on his back and got a good look at his face. "Manuel? Is that you?"

The Mexican's shirt was bloodied, likely from the blood that had flowed from his nose and mouth, Chance thought as he looked down at the man, who seemed barely alive. Still, through all of the blood, he knew it was Manuel. Before the man could answer, he picked him up as though he were nothing more than a feather and carried him over to Doc Riley's office.

Adam Riley was only a few years younger than Chance. He had settled in Twin Rifles just before the end of the War Between the States and taken up residency as the town physician. Like many a man of his profession in those days, he was qualified as a general physician and taught himself other aspects of doctoring as they arose. He had a good sense of humor and considered his first mission in life to be taking care of his patient the best he could.

"What did you do to this one, Chance, drag him in off the range?" he asked when Chance laid the Mexican down on the physician's bed. On more than one occasion, any one of the Carstons had been known to bring back men who were dead or close to dead from their exploits outside of Twin Rifles. At the moment, Manuel pretty much fit that description, Adam Riley thought.

"Believe it or not, he's a friend from down south," Chance said. "What he's doing here, I don't know, but he sure does look to be in bad shape."

"I'll say," was Doc Riley's reply once he got the

man's shirt off and gave him an initial examination. Aside from a broken nose and a bloody mouth, the man named Manuel had several large bruises on his side, each of them turning a dark purplish blue and tinged with an orange-colored red on the outskirts.

Chance stood by silently as Adam Riley worked his medical magic on the man, patching him up as best he could. A sniff of smelling salts revived the patient once he was through.

When Manuel saw Chance standing beside him, a wild look came over him. Still, it didn't stop him from getting out the words he had to say. He reached up and grabbed hold of Chance's arm, squeezed it hard and, in a frail voice, said, "Señor Chance. Señor Carston. You must come. It is José. They will kill him, they will kill all of them. Rosa, the *muchachos,* all of them." The look in his eyes grew wilder as he squeezed Chance's arm harder, enough so that the big man flinched. "You must come! You said you would." Then, in one final gasp, before lapsing back into unconsciousness, his voice weaker yet, he said, "You said you would."

When Chance had a confused look about him, Adam Riley looked at him and said, "Maybe now you can tell me what this is all about."

CHAPTER

Chance couldn't remember whether it had been three or four years since he had first met José Quesada, his wife, Rosa, their children, and Manuel. Time seemed to have gone so fast since the war had ended and he and Wash had returned to their home in Texas. The two brothers had settled on breaking wild mustangs for the army and had made a fair living at it.

"It was when we first got back from the war and got us some horses that we wound up meeting José and his brood," Chance said as Adam Riley poured the two of them coffee in his outer office. The doctor had determined that Manuel needed rest if nothing else and had decided to leave the man alone to sleep.

"I take it that was when you, your brother, and your

pa chased those horse thieves south of the border," Dr. Riley said as he sipped the strong black stuff.

Chance nodded, remembering the episode. "That it was."

He and Wash had made the mistake of hiring some ex-Confederate soldiers, men who had stuck around only long enough to steal the few head of horses the Carston brothers had. Chance would have followed them to hell and gone all by himself, but Wash and Pa had come along. There had also been a gunman by the name of Ben Thompson, who had tagged along for company. More than once he had come in handy when things got tough on that trip.

The Carstons had tracked the horses and the horse thieves to the corral of José Quesada, who had innocently agreed to hold them for the men who had recently stopped by his place. José and his wife had opened their home, a fair-sized adobe dwelling, to the Carstons and their friend. The man had even been instrumental in helping the Carstons finally catch the horse thieves. It was remembering all of this that Chance finally recalled that both he and his father had offered to help José and his family if the need ever arose. He said as much to Adam Riley.

"Sounds to me like your friend is calling in a marker," Doc Riley said, nodding toward the room Manuel now occupied.

"It would seem so," Chance agreed.

It would soon be suppertime and Chance offered to have a small meal brought up to Manuel. Adam Riley thanked the older Carston son as he left.

Normally, Chance would take his meals at the Ferris House, the town's only boardinghouse, which was run by a mother and daughter named Margaret and Rachel Ferris. Chance and Rachel had been exchanging romantic glances for some time now, even stealing a kiss from one another once in a while. But this afternoon he decided he would take his meal at the Porter Café, the only other eatery in town. It was run by Big John Porter and his daughter, Sarah Ann, who was also Chance's sister-in-law. He figured that since Sarah Ann had the recipe for the best fried chicken in town, she must also know how to make a good healthy broth for a man in need of it, a man like Manuel.

His brother Wash had come looking for him that afternoon and had decided to take his supper at the Porter Café. Chance took a seat across from him and explained what had happened concerning the arrival of Manuel and the condition he was in. When Sarah Ann took his order, he asked if she might brew up some chicken broth for a man who lay sick over at Doc Riley's.

Both brothers had fought in the War Between the States, Chance for the North and Wash for the South. When the occasion arose, both could still put up good arguments for why they had fought on the side that they had. On the other hand, both had learned that a good hot meal was something to be relished when it was offered to them, so when their food was served hardly a word was spoken as they proceeded to clear their plates in silence.

"Well, are you ready to go?" Sarah Ann asked after she had cleared their table and returned with a tray in her hand. The tray held little more than a spoon and a rather large bowl of what must have been soup or broth, covered with a checkered napkin.

"Oh, I can take it, Sarah Ann," Chance volunteered

in a somewhat humble manner. It was something he didn't often do when it came to dishes, for he firmly believed that dishes were a part of woman's work.

"Don't be silly," Sarah Ann said with a smile. "You'd spill half of it before you got to Doc Riley's. Besides, I asked Papa, and he said he could take care of the place if I wasn't gone too long."

When Chance had explained to Wash the mysterious arrival of Manuel, he hadn't gone into the reason the man had come to Twin Rifles. So he wasn't surprised to see the confused look on his brother's face when they entered Doc Riley's office and were introduced to Manuel, who was now very much awake.

In a seated position on his bed, Manuel alternately took grateful spoonfuls of Sarah Ann's chicken broth and repeated over and over to Wash and Chance, "You must come. You must come." He was still anxious to hear the Carston brothers say they would saddle and ride within the hour.

It only took Wash a minute or so to discover what was going on, once Chance reminded him of the horse thieves they had tracked down a few years back. Wash had the same questions as everyone else: What had happened to the man lying in bed before them? And exactly what was it he was so excited about?

Although he seemed to act much better once he had the broth in him, his level of excitement had remained the same. But Doc Riley knew that first things were first. And he, too, was as curious about Manuel as the Carstons.

"What I want to know, my friend, is just how you got in the shape you're in," he asked when Manuel was through eating. Both the Carston brothers and Sarah Ann were silent as they waited for the Mexican's explanation.

According to Manuel, his journey had not been a pleasant one. He had eagerly saddled José's best horse, enthusiastic in his desire to please his brother-in-law, and left as soon as possible. But he had ridden no more than ten miles when he was stopped by the very same *bandidos* who had just left José's abode. The three men—the tall *norteamericano,* the comanchero, and the tight-lipped Apache—had beaten him as badly if not worse than they had José. By the time they had finished beating his face in and kicking his ribs, they had warned him not to leave the area or something worse would happen to him and his family. Manuel had assured them he would not think of such a thing and lay there in pain as he watched them leave.

"I do not know if I make the right choice," he said, now out of breath in his urgency to get his story told. "The *norteamericano,* he is a mean one, I think, and if he wills bad upon us, I know it will be *muy mal,* very bad." A look of sadness came over him now as he looked first at Chance, then at Wash, and said, "José says you are men of your word, that you are Rangers *tejanos.* I hope he is right, for all the way up here, as much as I am in pain, something tells me, in here"—he slowly tapped his chest at this point—"that if you do not come, I will have no José and Rosa, no *muchachos,* when I return."

For Chance, there was no second thought as to what needed to be done about this man's predicament. There was fire in his eye as he looked directly at the Mexican and, in a voice filled with confidence, said,

"Don't you worry, amigo, we'll get the sons of bitches." Turning to his brother, he added, "Ain't that right, Wash?"

It was then that Sarah Ann quickly picked up her tray and bowl and rushed out of the room. It looked an awful lot like she was crying as she left.

CHAPTER

Margaret Ferris was refilling Will Carston's coffee cup when Big John Porter came barging into the dining area of the Ferris House. He took both Will and Margaret by surprise, for normally Big John could be found in his own establishment, the Porter Café. As the marshal of Twin Rifles, Will Carston was quick to notice that the huge man had an unpleasant look about him. It was a look that flat out scared the handful of customers who remained at the Ferris House community table. The only thing that seemed to soothe their shaken souls was the fact that Big John Porter was headed straight for Will Carston.

"My, what a surprise," Margaret said in a voice that was perhaps the calmest in the room. "I don't often get to see you, John." Like the perfect hostess she was,

Margaret Ferris was doing her utmost to be courteous to her customers, although Big John Porter had always been a competitor more than a customer of hers.

"Evening, Margaret. Looks like you're doing well," the proprietor of the Porter Café said in a voice that was more gravel than civilized tone in its composition. Without waiting for a reply, Big John turned to Will Carston, his voice dropping to a harder, much meaner timbre. "Will, what the hell's your boy been doing to my Sarah Ann?"

Will Carston finished his sip of coffee, set the cup down on the table in front of him, and rose to his full height. He wasn't as tall as Big John Porter, standing several inches over six feet, but the whole town knew he wouldn't take any guff from anyone, including Big John. Nor would he back down from a fight, which was what the man before him seemed headed for.

"Now, just what in the hell are you garbling about, John?" he said with as close to a snarl as you'd ever likely see Will Carston speak.

"Why, it's Sarah Ann! I send her off to Doc Riley's office with some soup for a patient of his and she comes back not half an hour later with a tray full of tears, mumbling how she hates Wash and Chance. Now, I want to know what's going on, damn it!"

"That being the case, why don't we ask these two culprits," Will said ever so calmly as his sons walked into the Ferris House. To Wash and Chance he said, "It appears you two got some tall explaining to do and you'd better do it quick, or I'll turn Big John loose on you."

"Sit down, boys—I'll get some more coffee," Margaret said before anyone else could get a word in edgewise. She had been serving meals to the Carstons long enough to know the temperament of each one of them. But since Will was in command of the situation, she knew it would be a long discussion before anyone threw a fist or pulled a gun. "You, too, John," she added in a commanding tone before disappearing into the kitchen.

Once the coffee was served, it took Chance a scant five minutes to explain what had happened that afternoon and Manuel's involvement in it.

"Then why's Sarah Ann crying like she just come back from my funeral?" Big John demanded.

"I'm afraid that's mostly my fault," Chance said with a sheepish smile.

"Not that I doubt your word, son, but just how is it your fault?" Will asked with a cocked eyebrow. If there was one thing Will Carston knew his oldest boy had, it was a penchant for getting into trouble.

"Well, I had to say we'd go, didn't I?" Chance blurted out, as though he had no other choice. "Hell, José told Manuel we were men of our word, Pa. Texas Rangers, he said! Do you know how long it's been since I've been told that?" There was a sincerity in his last words that expressed exactly how he felt, and both Will and Wash Carston knew the feeling well. The Texas Rangers had been disbanded during the middle of the War Between the States. All three of the Carstons had served with the Rangers for a number of years before the war and, if asked for an honest answer, would likely admit to missing the adventures they had once had as Texas Rangers. There was a certain amount of pride, not to mention a good deal of reputation, that went with being labeled a Texas Ranger. It stuck with a man most of his life if he was good as a Ranger, and Chance and Wash and Will had definitely been good Texas Rangers. "I couldn't turn him down, now, could I?"

"Maybe you couldn't, Chance, but that don't mean you got to make up everyone else's mind," Will said with a fatherly authority.

"He's got a point," Wash said. "It wasn't right, you putting me on the spot in front of Manuel like you did."

The scowl on Big John's face eased some as he began to understand what was going on between the Carston brothers and his daughter. "I reckon that explains Sarah Ann carrying on like she was." After a moment of thought, he looked Wash square in the eye and said, "You know, she ain't too fond of you traipsing off here and there and maybe getting shot up and all. I've got to tell you, Wash, she spends a lot of nights crying on my shoulder when you're gone like that. I hope you ain't gonna do this for a living, son. Breaking them mustangs is bad enough."

Will Carston saw that his youngest son was once again being put on the spot to make a decision and saw how uncomfortable it made him. The boy deserved better than that, he thought.

"What about you, Pa?" Chance asked. "You were there. You told José as much as I did to give a call if he needed it. Think you'd want to take a trip down south with me?"

Will shook his head regretfully. "Can't do it, son. Got them two Wade brothers over in the jail. Only seems a matter of who gets here first, the circuit judge or those boys they were riding with," Will said. "Fact of the matter is, I was thinking of asking your brother if he'd care to pin on a badge for the next week or two, just in case the *compadres* of those yahoos show up and want to dance."

Big John broke out with a smile. "Good. Then it's settled." Standing to his full height, Big John drained his coffee cup and turned to Margaret, who had stood aside with her coffeepot as the conversation took place. With a satisfied smile, he said, "Margaret, you brew the best coffee I've ever drank." He paused as Margaret blushed. "Except for mine, of course," he added as he left the Ferris House.

"Looks like it's me and Manuel on this trip," Chance said, his voice suddenly lacking any confidence. In fact, it was downright grim.

Wash finished his coffee and was on his feet when he said, "Good luck, Chance. I know you'll do a good job." If he sounded rather smug, it was because he meant to. It was about time Chance learned his lesson about volunteering him all the time.

Will was on his feet, too. He knew as well as Wash that Chance had talked himself into another peck of trouble. Still, the lad was his son and he shouldn't leave without giving him some words of encouragement. He slapped Chance on the shoulder, smiled, and said, "Look at it this way, son. It's only one gang of outlaws you're going after, right? You should be able to handle them without working up much of a sweat."

Chance sat there in a lonely state, watching his brother and father leave. And as he watched them, only one thought ran through his mind: Just how big was this gang Manuel was talking about?

CHAPTER

★ 5 ★

Chance rode into town early the next morning with Sarah Ann. Normally, she went to town early each morning to open up the Porter Café with Big John. She was in the habit of fixing a quick breakfast for Wash and Chance before she left, but this morning she only made Wash's meal. Even in the first dawn light that morning, Chance could see that she was upset at him over what had happened the previous day.

"I really didn't mean to distress you, Sarah Ann. I hope you know that," he said as she pulled her buckboard into the livery stable. Harvey Reed was there to take it for her, as courteous as could be. When Sarah Ann got married a couple of years back and continued to work at her father's eatery, Harvey had made a deal with her. He would keep her rig for her all day in his livery if she would provide a noon meal to him. It was an agreeable exchange for both parties, although recently Harvey had taken on Handy Partree, a strapping black man who did Harvey's blacksmith work and was capable of putting away a good-sized meal when he put his mind to it. Sarah Ann considered herself lucky that Handy didn't demand a heavy noon meal.

Sarah Ann began walking toward the Porter Café, at first totally ignoring Chance. After half a block of silence, she decided that she would have to face her brother-in-law sometime and get this out of her system.

"Chance, I don't think you truly know how much I love your brother or how much I fear for him when he's gone on those crazy schemes you Carstons get involved in," she said in a voice that bordered on angry.

Chance shrugged, again feeling helpless to a point. "What was I going to do, Sarah Ann? The man said his brother-in-law called us *men of honor*. After all, there's some things a man can't turn away from."

Sarah Ann continued to walk to the Porter Café, Chance walking the empty streets along with her. In her silence, she realized that there was a good deal of truth in what Chance was saying, for being a man of honor in this land meant quite a bit to most men out here. Still, sometimes she found herself wondering at the stupidity of the code these frontiersmen lived by all for some foolish belief in pride. It tended to make her mad when she realized that not only was her husband Wash a part of it, but that Chance was the one who kept him that way. Damn, but these men were stubborn sometimes!

"Well, Wash isn't going with you this time, Chance

Carston, and that's that," she said in an adamant tone as she reached the door to the Porter Café. "He thinks you've gotten yourself into one hellacious mess and so do I. All I hope is that you learn a lesson from taking on these outlaws, whoever they are. It's about time you realized that you are just as human as the rest of us." And with that Sarah Ann stuck her nose up in the air like some big-city snob and entered the Porter Café as though she had better things to do in her life than converse with her brother-in-law.

If being talked down to by Sarah Ann had been a surprise to Chance, he got another when he entered the Ferris House that morning. He knew that once Rachel discovered he would be leaving again, he could depend on her and Margaret to furnish him with a fair amount of supplies to take with him for a day or two. Past experience had taught him that even the leftovers the Ferris women served up were one hell of a lot better than any food a man could track down on the prairie once he left Twin Rifles. So part of his reason for eating here this morning was to gather up some grub to take along. But he wasn't at all prepared for what he saw as he entered the dining area that morning.

"Jesus, Mary, and Joseph," he muttered to himself at the sight of Manuel sitting there, wolfing down a huge meal. "What the hell are you doing here?" he added in amazement as he tossed his hat at the peg on the wall.

Manuel only smiled between mouthfuls of food. "These ladies, they cook almost as good as Rosa."

"I thought Doc Riley said you was bedridden at rest?"

Manuel slowly lifted his shoulders in indifference as

he shoveled more scrambled eggs into his mouth. Then, with another brief smile, he swallowed and said, "At another time, perhaps. But we must get back to José and Rosa and the *muchachos*. You do not forget they are in need of us, do you, señor?"

"No, of course not," Chance said in mild astonishment. "Spent half the night cleaning my Colt and my Spencer rifle. Gonna stop over to Kelly's Hardware soon as he opens up and load up on ammunition." At this point Chance pulled out his Colt conversion model .44, a new six-gun that he had managed to get a copy of before the actual production took place. As could be expected, Manuel was duly impressed with the sight of it. But then most folks south of the border were real impressed with American firearms anyway.

"You kill many *bandidos* with this weapon, eh?" Manuel said, his eyes wide with amazement as he took in the Colt's features.

"I try, Manuel." Chance smiled. It was likely as close to being humble as Chance would ever get.

Rachel soon stood before him, a slight frown about her as she poised her pencil to take his order. "I hear you're leaving again," she said in a none-too-thrilled voice.

"I'll take whatever my amigo had plus an extra side of meat," Chance said, ignoring her statement. There was total silence as Rachel wrote down the order, then stared back down at Chance, the frown on her forehead broadening somewhat. "Yeah, I'm leaving, Rachel. Heading south of the border for a while. Owe Manuel and his family a favor or two."

"I see," Rachel said, and was gone. In a moment she returned with a coffee cup for Chance. She filled the cup, then proceeded to refill Manuel's cup. All of this was done in silence. It was when she was through that she gave the Mexican a hard look as she said, "Wherever it is you're taking him, señor, you'd better make sure I get him back alive." The frown on her face deepened as she turned her gaze to Chance and added, "Now I'm beginning to understand how Sarah Ann feels about all of this."

Then she was gone.

Chance ate his meal in relative silence, especially when Rachel was around with that pot of coffee. A woman could be devilish mean with a coffeepot in her hands, and Rachel was angry enough to do something with it if the mood struck her. So Chance ate his meal and tried to ignore Rachel, as much as he was tempted o take in her beautiful features.

"She has the eye for you, that one," Manuel said with a hint of a smile as he watched Rachel head for he kitchen. "Someday she will make you an honest man, no?"

"That seems to be her line of thought," Chance eplied, and finished his meal.

"Are the others waiting outside?" Manuel asked when Chance toyed with his cup as though he had omething on his mind.

"There ain't no others, amigo—just you and me."

"But—"

"Pa and Wash would have come along but they got other business they got to take care of," Chance said. t wasn't exactly a lie, just stretching the truth a mite, Chance reasoned with himself. "So like I say, it's just ou and me."

"But, Señor Chance—"

"Your horse is down at the livery. I had him fed and ubbed down last night. Long as we don't push him oo hard, he should be all right for a good day's ride. Why don't you go get him? I'll meet you out front."

Chance was very intentional about what he wanted Manuel to do. But the Mexican recognized the man's troubles and knew he needed to be left alone. With a nod of assent he was soon gone from the table and the Ferris House.

Chance walked into the kitchen as though he owned the place, not really caring what Margaret might think of so bold a move. It was Rachel he had to see now and he was hoping Margaret would have the good sense to leave the room to take care of some chore, real or imagined. Out of the corner of his eye he saw Margaret give him a sour look before disappearing from the kitchen area.

"Visitor, honey," she said as she walked out the door.

It suited Chance fine, for when Rachel spun around she was looking straight at him. He took her in his arms and kissed her with a passion he hadn't felt for some time. When she pushed him away, he wasn't sure whether it was because she still had work to do at the stove she was slaving over or whether she wanted to not be near him.

"I don't know if I can stand this anymore, Chance," she said in a breathless tone, as though she were getting the words out while trying to take in a breath of air.

"Stand what?"

She thought he seemed genuinely confused. "Every time you leave it gets worse. The waiting, not knowing when you'll be back or *if* you'll be back. Not knowing what to think—"

"Been talking to Sarah Ann again, ain't you?"

"As a matter of fact, yes," Rachel said, the fire coming back to her now. "And what she said makes sense. Waiting like that can make a woman a nervous wreck."

"Oh, horse apples," Chance said, dismissing her words. "I've known Wash all my life and he can take care of himself fine."

"Don't you see it, you fool!" she said, and grabbed his arms, pulling him to her. "What Sarah Ann feels for Wash, well, I feel the same thing for you." This time it was she that kissed him in a passionate way. And as every other time she had done it to him, the action left Chance a bit more than befuddled.

"Don't worry, Rachel, I found out there's only three of them outlaws," Chance said, not knowing what in the world else he could possibly say that would make sense. For the moment it seemed to placate her fears.

But it was as he was walking out the doors of the Ferris House that his own words came back to haunt him. Manuel had described three *bandidos:* an Apache Indian, a comanchero, and a man he only described as a *norteamericano.* What he was wondering as he left was just how many friends those three *bandidos* had. There was no telling about the *norteamericano*—he could be alone or with friends. As for the Apache and the comanchero, he was sure each one had a lot of other friends. A whole lot of other friends.

CHAPTER

The sun had been up for nearly an hour by the time Kelly's Hardware opened up. Chance was the first customer Kelly had and was able to get the needed ammunition he knew he would require for this trip. He decided he'd better pick up more than he thought he would need.

Manuel didn't have a six-gun on him—only the rifle he had carried with him when he'd ridden into Twin Rifles. Weapons expertise was one of Chance Carston's fortes, so it only took a once-over to know that the Sharps conversion model Manuel was carrying would be sufficient for long-distance shooting, but that was about all. The rifle was still a single shot and took time to reload. If they got into the thick of it with the *federales* or comancheros or any of the various

Indian tribes that roamed south of the border, well, the Sharps wouldn't be much good for more than a club past that first shot. And Chance had that strange inkling in the back of his mind that this trip was going to be one whole lot more dangerous than any of his previous ones. So he bought a goodly amount of ammunition for the Sharps, figuring that if Manuel didn't use it on the *bandidos* he would at least have some good target-practice ammunition.

He was about to pay the bill for the extra ammunition he'd bought for his Colt revolver when Kelly informed him that his supply of ammunition for the Spencer rifle was getting mighty low. This struck a chord in Chance's mind and as an afterthought he picked up a box of .44s for a Henry rifle.

"Taking a Henry along with you, too?" Kelly asked out of curiosity. Like everyone else in Twin Rifles, Kelly knew that when Chance Carston went off to war, he went off ready to bring back the whole bear—hide, snout, and all.

"No. It just crossed my mind I'd likely need 'em after all," was Chance's reply as Kelly shrugged noncommittally and added them to the sum total of the bill.

They headed south out of town, taking their time, although it was easy to see that Manuel wanted to ride the horses into the ground to get to José and Rosa and those kids. Not that Chance or anyone else could blame the man. As Chance recalled, Manuel had gotten along real well with his brother-in-law, his sister, and their kids. And from the way Manuel was acting, it was evident that the man still felt a great deal of compassion for the family he lived with. It was doubtful that he would have ridden as far and as fast as he had to get hold of the Carstons if he didn't.

Yet there was still the thought in the back of Chance's mind that they were going to need more than the two of them to clean up this mess, especially if what Manuel had said was anywhere close to the truth. And Manuel didn't impress Chance as a teller of tall tales. After all, if there were only three of them, as Manuel had described, why, there wouldn't be any difficulty taking care of those yahoos in proper order. It wouldn't be the first time he had taken on more than two or three at a time and managed to survive the ordeal.

The worst part of this whole adventure was that he had gone and promised his help before he'd actually known how many men he would be facing, and Pa and Wash wouldn't be there to back him up if something went wrong. Although he would never admit it to anyone, Chance Carston felt a chill run down his spine and it was scary as hell. Oh, he could take care of himself all right. Hell, hadn't he made it through four years of that damned war without Pa or his brother at his side? And that had been some of the fiercest fighting he had done in his life.

This newfound fear, the idea that he might not come back alive, just as Rachel had suggested, set him to wondering if perhaps he wasn't getting to be older than he was acting. Maybe it was time to settle down like Pa was always harping on him to do, like Wash had tried to do when he married Sarah Ann. But Sarah Ann was right—he kept luring his brother back into those fights, back into those dangerous situations where either or both of them could wind up dying for nothing. He knew that there was time enough to think about all of this. But at the moment, the foremost thought in his mind was, who could he get to come along on this trek? Who would be crazy enough to throw in with this sorry outfit and be willing to travel south of the border to save the skin of a man and his family he didn't even know?

They were an hour out of Twin Rifles when Chance got his answer.

They came upon half a dozen horses on the open prairie, half of them ground tied as they stood around several men who had congregated. Chance undid the thong on his Colt and lifted it out of the holster, gently dropping it back in its seat when he saw who it was he was riding up on.

"What are you up to, Wilson?" he asked Wilson Hadley as he rode up to the group of men. Carny Hadley, Wilson's brother, was lying on the ground, obviously in pain. From the looks of it, he had fallen on his leg—or something had fallen on his leg. Sprained or busted, Chance bet. Next to him, down on one knee, was Ike Hadley, one of the younger Hadley brothers. He looked worried more than anything. Wilson had simply been cussing under his breath as Chance and Manuel had ridden up.

"Carny, the damn fool, had it in mind to break a horse," Wilson growled, looking down at his brother with a frown. "Seems the horse broke him."

"How bad?"

"Busted his leg, I think. You think that town doctor would be able to take care of this?" Wilson asked.

The Hadley brothers and the Carston boys had never seen eye to eye. In fact, they had grown up trying to beat the living tar out of one another, acting as though all of them were mortal enemies. And up until the time of the war they pretty much had been. But when the war came the five Hadley brothers and the Carstons had gone their separate ways, not renewing their relationships until the war was over. Wilson and Carny, the two oldest Hadleys, still had an occasional run-in with Chance and Wash Carston, but nothing like they used to have as young boys. Besides, the Carstons had been too busy breaking horses for the army to get into much trouble with the Hadleys, who lived to the south of town. The truth was, Wilson and Carny had come in right handy in a couple of instances these past couple of years, helping out some people in town who were needing it. The fact that one of those people had been Sarah Ann gave Chance and Wash a more tolerable outlook on the Hadleys. Chance even found himself feeling a bit of compassion for Carny as he dismounted.

"By the time you git back to town to get a buckboard, he's likely to worsen," Chance said to Wilson.

"That's what I figure," Wilson said. Chance almost expected the man to take a poke at him, but all he could do was stand there as helplessly as the rest of them.

"Me too." It was a familiar voice to Chance but it sounded out of place out here—out of place among the Hadleys. When he looked over his shoulder, Chance saw Dallas Bodeen making his way toward camp, dragging a couple of heavy limbs from a nearby tree under his arms. "He don't get looked at by a professional man right quick, I figure he'll be on his way to a swift grave."

"Is he gonna die?" a worried Ike Hadley asked.

"Aw, shut up, Ike, you worthless brat," Wilson growled at his brother.

"I doubt it, son," Dallas said in his genial way placing a steady hand on Ike's shoulder. The lad couldn't have been more than seventeen, but that didn't bother Dallas, for he could remember starting out his own life as a mountain man at that age. "Not if we can get us a travois hooked up to one of these horses and you and your brother can get him back to town pronto. Doc Riley—he's a good man when it comes to fixing a body up. You take my word for it."

The mountain man in Dallas seemed to be prepared for just about anything. Using extra buckskin ties from his saddlebags, he and Chance rigged up a serviceable travois while Wilson Hadley knelt next to his brother and offered him assurances of help soon being at hand. Carny let out a piercing scream as they moved him to the travois, then he passed out from the intense pain in his leg.

Chance watched the Hadleys as they headed for Twin Rifles, Carny lying on their makeshift travois. For an instant what caught his eye was Ike Hadley, who was looking over his shoulder at Chance, Manuel, and Dallas Bodeen. But he couldn't for the life of him figure out what was on the boy's mind.

"Well, now, Chance, what are you doing this far south?" Dallas asked. "And who's your friend?"

Once again Chance told the story of how Manuel had come to Twin Rifles and what he had come for. He also went into a bit of background on how he had first met José, Rosa, and Manuel several years ago. "Man helped me get my horses back and I told him if he was ever in need—"

Dallas held up the palm of his hand to stop Chance from having to feel any more humble than he likely already did. "Know what you mean, old hoss. Done it a time or two my own self."

"Well, I reckon we better be going," Chance said in a rather uncomfortable way.

"Say, ain't you boys a mite shorthanded for taking on a chore like you're talking about?" Dallas said, the reins of his horse in his hand, although he had yet to mount. "I mean, them comancheros—why, they's thick as fleas, you know. And it ain't just the Apache down there either. Tonkawas and that raving Kickapoo tribe, too, from what I hear tell."

"Is that right?" It had crossed his mind as soon as he'd seen old Dallas that he could use him on this trek. The man had spent a good deal of his life up in the mountains with Will Carston before the two of them had become Texas Rangers, not long after the fur trade had died out. Chance had a working knowledge of the Comanche Indians, for they seemed to be everywhere in Texas, but he would openly confess to not knowing much about the other tribes that roamed the area, particularly the ones south of the border, where they were headed. Dallas, on the other hand, seemed to know more about the Indians everywhere than, well, most of the Indians everywhere. "You wouldn't be volunteering for a ride down south, would you? Sure could use a man as good with Indian sign as you are, Dallas."

Dallas pushed his hat back on his head and scratched it in thought. "Well, now, let me see." He lifted an arm and sniffed at his armpit. "Nope. Ain't due for a bath for another couple of weeks. I reckon that only leaves me short of one thing."

"What's that?"

"Why, ammunition for my Henry, of course!" the old mountain man said, as though Chance should know exactly what he was talking about.

At this Chance smiled an ear-to-ear grin. Reaching back, he undid the tie on one of the saddlebags, dug out two boxes of .44s, and tossed one, then the other, to Dallas Bodeen.

"Not anymore, Dallas," he said, his smile still present.

When he gave a wink to Manuel, he could see that the Mexican was a whole lot more comfortable with the situation.

CHAPTER

★ 7 ★

The three of them rode another twenty miles before making a dry camp at noon. The riding had been easy so far and Chance was sure they would reach the Rio Grande by the time the day was over.

"Looks like Miss Margaret's biscuits," Dallas said with a grin as Chance tossed him one when they took time for a meal, the contents of which were little more than a biscuit and some water. The further south they got the more dry camps they would be making, he was sure.

"That's a fact," Chance said as he tossed a biscuit to Manuel and kept one for himself. As he had suspected, Rachel and Margaret had managed to scrape together some extra leftovers for him once they knew he was leaving town again.

"Oh, the ladies who run the inn," Manuel said, fondly remembering their food. He took a bite of the biscuit, nodded, and said, "Yes, this belongs to them."

"I swear they could round up enough grub to feed an army on a moment's notice if they were called to," Dallas offered around a mouthful of biscuit.

"But you ever notice how contradictory they get?"

"How's that, Chance?" Dallas made quick work of finishing his biscuit, swallowing what was left with a gulp of tepid water.

"Take Rachel, for example. Tells me this morning she's taking on Sarah Ann's belief that I'm supposed to stop this traipsing around the country like I been doing. Claims she's sure that one of these days I ain't gonna come back alive."

"What's your point?" Dallas asked, picking what was left of his teeth.

Chance spread his hands out, palms up, and said, "Why, if they just *know* I ain't coming back, what in the devil are they loading me down with three days' worth of food for? Want to make sure I don't dwindle away to nothing before I meet my Maker, do they?"

Dallas chuckled to himself. "It 'pears to me they just ain't giving up on you much as they say they are. You know, the way to a man's heart is supposed to be through his stomach, or so I hear."

"Sí." Manuel nodded and slowly drank his water. "I have heard this. You ask Rosa and she will tell you. It is how she has kept José home these many years."

"It's all a conspiracy, if you ask me," Chance said, then arose, put away his mess gear, and saddled up to ride. Neither of the other two questioned his movements as anything but a silent command to ride on. Both seemed to be comfortable with Chance in the role of leader of this expedition. After all, he had spent nearly as much time as Dallas in the Texas Rangers and, by Dallas's own admission, was a whale of a shot and a better-than-average fighter.

So if Chance was wanting to lead them into Mexico and a hazardous mission, well, let him. The man was acting as though this were some sort of personal vendetta anyway, as far as Dallas was concerned. And arguing with Chance was about the same as arguing with a mule or a cook, and everyone west of the Mississippi knew that only a fool argued with a mule or a cook. And Dallas Bodeen was no fool, by God!

A good share of this part of Texas was what you called brush country, but the brush started to thin out the farther south you went and it did just that by late afternoon. Chance had been right about their traveling distance and they had come on the Rio Grande at one of its thinner crossings about an hour before sundown. The river separating the territorial United States—the state of Texas in particular—and the country of Mexico couldn't have been more than fifty to seventy-five feet wide where they would cross the next morning.

Years ago, when Texas had obtained statehood, there had been a good deal of confusion and argument over the true border of Texas and Mexico. Texans claimed it was the Rio Grande River. But the Mexican government, fighting until the last to get every bit of ground it could, maintained that it was the Nueces River. The two governments had finally settled on the Rio Grande, but if that wasn't enough there was always the fact that the river itself tended to change course each year, depending on the amount of rainfall it received on a yearly basis.

"Don't recall this crossing," Chance said as he dismounted at the Rio Grande that afternoon.

"Didn't you say you was chasing horses last time?" Dallas said. Out of habit he loosened his cinch and let the horse blow before letting it drink the cool river water.

"Yeah."

"God only knows where you crossed then, hoss. Keeping track of a herd of horses ain't the easiest thing in the world, you know, whether they's stolen or not."

"Sí," Manuel said in agreement. Although he desperately wanted to get back to his home in Mexico, he was secretly glad that Chance had slackened the pace once they had started out. The doctor had told Manuel that he must not ride too hard or all the wrapping of his ribs would be of little use to him. The idea was to keep the ribs in place so they could heal the way they were supposed to. And by the end of the day, Manuel knew exactly what the good doctor in Twin Rifles had been talking about.

Luckily, the land had been fairly free of obstructions and the group was still able to cover a decent amount of distance that day. Still, pain and all, he tried to find some humor in the day's events. With a forced smile, Manuel added, "I do not think I have ever crossed this river in the same place more than once—she changes that much. She is like a fickle woman—she cannot make up her mind where she wants to go."

Chance and Dallas laughed softly and began to make camp.

Dallas dug around in Chance's saddlebags and found some of the supplies the Ferris women had provided him. Dallas had been around the Carston brothers long enough to know that Chance couldn't cook worth spit and would likely starve to death if he was on the trail by himself. Dallas was fixing up some rather thick slices of bacon when Manuel joined him at the fire, producing a small fry pan and a bag of beans.

"Mexican strawberries, huh?" Dallas grumbled. "Thought I'd seen the last of them some years back. But I forgot which direction we're heading in. I'll pass on them, amigo. You make some and share 'em with Chance ary you want. Coffee, bacon, a biscuit, and some sopping grease will do just fine for me, thank you."

"I understand, señor. Sometimes the constitution is not so firm," Manuel said with a nod.

Dallas let the comment pass and was silent throughout the rest of the meal. As Dallas had suggested, Manuel offered some of his beans to Chance, who willingly filled his plate with them. Along with the bacon and a biscuit, he thought he had a veritable feast for supper that night. And true to form he was quick in gulping down the meal. It was a good thing, too, for it was coming on dark when Chance heard a rider coming toward their camp. He still had his cup of coffee in hand and had stood to his full height, undoing the thong on his holstered Colt as the stranger galloped toward their fire.

To his bewilderment, Chance saw that it was Ike Hadley who rode into camp. The boy and the horse looked as though they had ridden hard to get to the Rio Grande. However, Chance could have sworn the edges of Ike's mouth were turned up in a partial smile as he pulled to a halt. Ike dismounted, uncinched his horse, and gave it a swat on the rump, sending it to the river to drink deep.

"This close to dark you could get killed pulling a stunt like that," Chance said, taking out his revolver hefting it, giving Ike Hadley a hard look, and then replacing the six-gun in its holster. Riding into camp, anyone's camp, without so much as a "hello the camp" wasn't the safest thing to do in this land.

But Chance's words apparently went unnoticed. Ike was indeed smiling as he said, "Carny and Wilson keep saying I'm too gangly to miss riding in the saddle."

"Must be some truth to it, I reckon," Chance grudgingly admitted. "Hell, ugly as they are, it's pretty damn hard to miss either Carny or Wilson, on horse or afoot."

"Ary you got you a cup and a plate, I reckon we might be able to git old Manuel to fix up a mess of them strawberries he's infected Chance with tonight." Dallas had been through enough hard times in his ife to know that it was best to start off on a friend-y note with a virtual stranger, no matter who he night be.

"Thank you, Mr. Bodeen," Ike Hadley said as he quietly made his way to his horse and fished around in iis saddlebags for the required implements before eturning to the campsite. That Ike was much quieter han his brothers was one of the first things Dallas had ioticed when he'd come upon Carny and his broken eg and his brother just standing there cussing a blue treak. It appeared the boy had manners, too.

Chance squinted at Ike in the evening dusk, watch-ng the boy both going to the river and returning. Ike adn't filled out in the husky manner that his bigger rothers had and, at the age of seventeen, still had a ays to go to be a full-fledged Hadley, he thought. But t wasn't Ike's build that was bothering Chance right ow. No, there was something else—something that ade Ike look out of place at the moment.

"Ain't that Carny's gun you're wearing, son?" he asked when the young Hadley had returned to camp.

Even by the bright light of the fire, Chance could plainly see that Ike was blushing now. Must have stolen it, Chance thought to himself.

"Yeah, what about it?" Trying to sound tough, just like Carny and Wilson.

"How'd you come on it?"

Dallas tried to save the boy some embarrassment by handing him a cup of coffee while Manuel fixed more beans. "You must have rid mighty hard to git here in the time you did. Last time I seen you, why, you was headed for Twin Rifles and we was near an hour out of town."

"Yes, sir." Ike took a careful sip of the black stuff—the only cup of it left in the pot, whether he knew it or not—and added, "Wilson figured he was tired of me asking whether Carny was gonna die. Got meaner than usual and told me to get the hell out of there. I reckon we was halfway to Twin Rifles."

"Well, why didn't you go home, son? You Hadleys got you a cabin of sorts out there someplace, don't you?" Dallas asked, a note of concern in his voice.

Ike took another healthy sip of his coffee. A sour look came to his face and it wasn't from the taste of the coffee. "You don't understand, Mr. Bodeen. Wilson just claimed I was worthless as could be. Told me to git. Said he didn't want to see me again. Not at home, not nowhere." His face looked as sad as he sounded now as he turned to Chance. "That's how I got Carny's gun. Scared of Wilson as I am, I ain't about to head off into this wilderness without a gun and all I had was a run-down Ballard rifle. Wilson stopped his horse and travois, pulled Carny's gun off of him, and said Carny would likely die anyway. He shoved it at me and said he never wanted to see me again." At these last words it was evident that Ike Hadley was on the verge of tears.

"Great—now I've got to baby-sit a snot-nosed kid," Chance grumbled.

"No." Ike sounded stubborn now. "That ain't why I come along—you got to know that, Mr. Carston." He set the cup on the ground, wiped his nose with a sleeve, and stood to his full height. He was a few inches shorter than Chance, but he didn't like being talked down to any more than anyone else did in these parts. "There's only one reason I ever seen you ride by us and that was on your way to git into some kind of difficulty, Mr. Carston. There ain't nothing back at that cabin for me. Fact is, the only reason I come along now is because I want to prove to Wilson that what he says ain't true. Not one bit."

"And you think getting yourself killed is gonna prove something to Wilson?" Chance asked in a snarl. "Only thing it's gonna prove to him, kid, is that you're as stupid as he claims you are. Go back home, kid—"

"You son of a bitch!" Ike growled.

Chance never finished what he was saying.

Ike was just as much a hothead as his older brothers and was going for his gun—Carny's gun. But by the time he had it out, Chance had grabbed a huge fist around the cylinder, sticking a finger down in between the hammer and the cylinder so it wouldn't fire. At the same time he was also poking his Colt conversion model .44 into Ike's gut. All he had to do was pull the trigger and Ike would be dead, and from the looks on both of their faces, they both knew it.

"You'd better smile real wide when you say that,

sonny, or there's two things you'll never do again," Chance said in a hard voice, his steely eyes burning into those of Ike Hadley.

"What's that?" Ike stuttered.

"You'll never call me a son of a bitch again and you'll never smile again." At the same time he holstered his own revolver, Chance pulled Ike's from his grip. God only knew what would happen next.

"The *frijoles* are ready, señor," Manuel said from out of nowhere.

Dallas grabbed Ike Hadley by the shoulder and physically plunked him down on the ground next to Manuel, who was soon spooning beans onto the lad's plate. "That's right—don't want the boy to eat cold food now, do we?"

"Dallas—" Chance started to say.

"Chance, I firmly believe that this is something we need to sleep on tonight, don't you?" Dallas said. "All of us."

Chance was mad enough to fight even Dallas at this point, but when he looked up at the old mountain man, he got humble real quick. For there was Dallas holding that Henry rifle of his in the crook of his arm and it was aimed right at Chance's chest.

"Sure. All of us should sleep on it," was all Chance said.

CHAPTER

★ 8 ★

eremiah Younger had a sad look about him. Seated at he community table at the Ferris House, he didn't eem to be enjoying his breakfast meal at all. He had urposely come in late, hoping to miss the normal rowd who ate their morning meal at the Ferris Iouse. The truth was, he simply didn't feel like alking to anyone—not with the problems he had.

"Why, Mr. Younger, you're not sick or anything, are ou?" Margaret asked, a note of concern in her voice. efilling his coffee cup, she had seen him do little iore than push the home-fried potatoes and eggs round on his plate. "It's not our food, is it?"

"No, of course not, dear lady." Younger was sudenly quite embarrassed over the way he had been acting. "You serve excellent food. I'm afraid it's my appetite that has left me temporarily."

"Ain't been out here long, have you, friend?" Will Carston had never been one to ask an inarticulate question or hold back an opinion. The way he saw it, why, it was all part of being a lawman. The morning meal had been served up and most of the customers were now gone, Will Carston and Jeremiah Younger being the only two left at the community table.

"I beg your pardon, sir?" the gambler asked with a frown.

"Margaret serves up the best meals you're likely to eat this side of the Pecos," Will said with a good deal of pride. "You travel West of the Pecos and you'll need to get clear to one of them fancy eateries in San Francisco to match the taste of this food. And that's a fact."

"Your point, sir?"

"Why, I was you, I'd eat ary what Miss Margaret puts before me," Will said with a tone that was filled with astonishment, the astonishment being that Mr. Younger wasn't aware of this fact by now. Every word he'd spoken of Margaret Ferris's culinary abilities was the truth, as could be attested to by anyone in Twin Rifles who had eaten her cooking. "I expect any day now someone's gonna taste her vittles and propose marriage to her on the spot."

"Oh, go on, Will." Margaret smiled as a blush worked its way into her already rosy cheeks.

"I'll keep that in mind, sir," Younger said as Will pushed himself away from the table, sloshed on his hat, and left.

Margaret disappeared into the kitchen for only a moment and reappeared with a coffee cup. She set it

lown opposite Jeremiah Younger, poured herself
ome of the hot liquid, and took a seat.

"There really is something bothering you, isn't
here?" Margaret Ferris had tended enough sick men
n her lifetime to try to see herself as a humanitarian
of sorts. She had likely heard more hard-luck stories
han Ernie Johnson, and she had heard them from
oth men and women alike. Therefore, she did her
est to try and listen to those who were feeling sad
bout something, like Mr. Younger apparently was,
nd dispense some worthwhile advice once she found
ut what the trouble was. "I mean, I was only joshing
bout the food."

"No, madam, I'm afraid my troubles go a bit deeper
han your friend's opinion of your culinary art,"
eremiah Younger said. "Much deeper."

"Oh, come on, things can't be that bad," Margaret
aid, trying to be encouraging. "Can they?"

When Jeremiah Younger poured his problems out
o Margaret, they came as though a dam had burst
nside the man, and she thought she sensed a genuine
eeling of relief in Younger as he poured out his sad
ale. Like many who now resided in Texas, Jeremiah
ounger had come from somewhere else. In his case, it
as a small city in Illinois. He and his wife had never
tarted a family and now he was a widower. He had
ever been all that successful at the general store he
wned and ran, so one day he took a friend's advice
nd struck out to do what he wanted to in life. After
ll, the friend had said, life was too short.

Jeremiah had taken an interest in cards at an early
ge and found himself rather dexterous with a deck of
asteboards. On a riverboat headed for New Orleans,
e had watched the professional gamblers every night,

finally engaging one to show him the more promising card tricks. By the time he had reached New Orleans, he not only could play a decent game of cards but hold his own against the gamblers.

"I drifted from town to town for a while, finally coming to your fair metropolis," he concluded. "I'm afraid I'm still not as good with a deck of cards as I thought I was, though, for a rather husky man caught me cheating at the old shell game the other day. I fear it has ruined my reputation in this town. He suggested I find a new profession, and I'm afraid he is right. Face it, madam, I'm little more than a failure."

A failure? Of course, how couldn't he feel that way? The man had lost the only woman he had ever loved, then given up a good solid business for the life of a drifter. He was probably down to little more than what he could pay for a week's worth of lodging at the Ferris House and maybe a stagecoach ticket out of town. Add to that the fact that he'd just been exposed as a cheat and, yes, he was pretty much a failure. Margaret didn't have any immediate answer to Jeremiah Younger's problem, but what she did know was that the man was desperately in need of someone who believed in him.

"Listen, Mr. Younger, everything is gonna be all right," she said with a confident smile. "I just know it is—believe me."

For the first time in two days, Jeremiah Younger's face sported a smile of its own. He placed a slender hand on Margaret's and gave it a gentle squeeze. "Somehow I know that beauty such as you possess would never be capable of lying, so I will believe you, my dear."

"Good. Now, the first thing you've got to do is not sit around and feel sorry for yourself," Margaret said in her cheeriest voice. "Be active. Do things." She snapped her fingers, as though an idea had just come to mind. "I've got it. You can help me out today for starters."

"Really?" he said, genuinely surprised. "But how could I do that? You ladies do such a credible job of running this place that I doubt I could ever—"

Margaret took a gulp of her coffee and said, "Listen, Mr. Younger—"

"Call me Jeremiah, please."

"Fine, Jeremiah. Rachel has got her hands full with the noon meal and I'm going to really have more than I can do to get the supper meal going."

Jeremiah seemed puzzled. "But I'm no cook—how could I help you?"

"How do you feel about serving a meal?" Margaret asked.

As it turned out, Margaret had gotten word of Carny Hadley and his broken leg. Contrary to what Wilson might have thought, his brother hadn't died, although Carny would be bedridden for some time until his leg had healed properly. Adam Riley had seen Margaret yesterday afternoon and asked the proprietress of the Ferris House if she or Rachel would be able to bring three meals a day to Carny Hadley. Margaret had just remembered the promised meals while she had been talking to Jeremiah. The whole idea seemed to be a blessing in disguise, for not only would she be able to use the extra time she needed to prepare her meals—she and Rachel really were going to be busy taking care of meals for the next day or two—but Jeremiah would begin to feel like a useful human being and perhaps start to work out his own problems. The only real problem she would have was trying to make her guarantee that "everything would be all right" come true for Jeremiah. That, she told herself, could be a chore and a half.

Jeremiah drew a lot of attention that morning as he walked from the Ferris House to nearly the other side of town. As tall and gangly as he was, that might have been nothing out of the ordinary, but this morning he was carrying a tray full of plates and a pot of coffee. Carny Wilson, after all, was no small man and had an appetite almost as big as his mouth.

Adam Riley thanked Jeremiah, assuring him that he would run up a bill for the food, which would be part of what he would charge Carny Hadley once he was released from his care. In fact, when he left the doctor's office Jeremiah felt a real sense of accomplishment. Having released Margaret Ferris to do other things in her business made him feel almost as useful as he had during the early years of his marriage when he had taken great joy in helping out his wife around their house.

"Look at that, will you, Sam?" one of the men not halfway up the block said as they stepped out in front of him. "He not only acts like a fool but looks like one as well."

"I beg your pardon, sir?" Jeremiah said as he came to an abrupt halt, the tray filled with empty plates balanced in his left hand.

"Seen you walking down the street not long ago," Sam said. He was a tall man, more solid in build than Jeremiah. A sneer came to his face as he added, "Say Harry, maybe we should get him a wig and make him look like a woman. Sure ain't seen no one but a waitress carry a serving plate, and he don't look nothing like no female I ever seen, huh?"

Harry had silently worked his way over to

Jeremiah's side and gave him a shove, pushing him toward the entrance to an alley. The gambler stumbled sideways and fell into the side of a building, what plates he had on his tray clattering to the ground noisily.

"Please, gentlemen, I'm not looking for a fight," he said as he tried to regain his balance. He didn't sound any too brave about his proposition either, which apparently egged these two ruffians on the more.

Harry pushed him hard again and Jeremiah lost his balance, once more falling further into the alley and its darkness. He had never seen these two before, but one thing Jeremiah did know was that they were nothing more than bullies. Perhaps he had played cards with them a few days back and they had lost and he didn't remember. God only knew there were enough sore losers in the world. He had found that out on the riverboat. Still, he couldn't remember them or their faces and didn't know why they had picked on him to bully around. All he knew was he didn't like it one bit.

It was when that thought passed through his mind that he recalled the get-up that the professional gambler had told him to make a part of his daily attire. Jeremiah had never really approved of violence but from the look of these two roughs, he was about to get a dose of it real fast.

"I wouldn't do that, my friend," he said when the one called Sam readied to throw a punch at him. Jeremiah's arm shot out as he spoke and he suddenly got the impression that it wasn't his words these two were paying attention to so much as it was the derringer in his outstretched hand. It was a .41-caliber hideout with an over-and-under barrel combination, just enough to put one well-placed slug in each of these men and make them remember it the rest of their lives. "I could kill you here and now if I chose."

"Now what the devil's going on here?" the voice of Will Carston said as he made his way across the street. He had heard the rattling sound of the dishes falling to the ground and decided to investigate. The only place he was used to hearing that sound was inside the Porter Café or the Ferris House. By the time he reached Jeremiah and the two ruffians, the derringer was out of sight. "Some kind of accident we got here, is it?" he asked when he arrived on the scene.

"Two of your town bullies thought I was easy prey," Jeremiah said with as much authority as he could muster.

"Hell, Marshal, you should have seen what this man was about to do to us," the one called Harry said.

Will glanced down at the ground and the broken plates. Next he took in the two ruffians, who were wearing six-guns, then Jeremiah, who was apparently unarmed.

"And just what was it you was about to do to these pillars of society, Mr. Younger?" Will asked, already having made up his mind as to what had gone on here.

"This," Jeremiah said, and quickly brought the side of the tray up alongside Harry's head, knocking his hat off and banging him hard enough to cause a ringing sensation in the man's head.

"Well, boys, I think from what I see here that it's time for you two to pay up," Will said when Jeremiah had the tray at his side again.

"What the hell for?" Sam asked in an indignant tone.

"Boys, I'd bet a dollar them plates belong to Miss Margaret. Now, you make up your mind whether you want to pay for 'em here and now or wash her dishes for a month or so. And believe me, boys, I can make you do it," Will said, thumbing the badge on his chest.

Sam dug into his pockets and pulled out some coins, dropping several of them in Will Carston's hand until the marshal was satisfied Margaret Ferris would have enough to buy new plates with. Then he handed it over to Jeremiah.

"I assume you was delivering food over to Carny Hadley for Miss Margaret?" he said.

"Yes, Marshal."

"Well, you clean this mess up and take it back to her. Tell her that coinage ought to buy her twice as many plates as you got broke. Make you look good to her, it will."

"Yes, Marshal."

Jeremiah did just as the lawman said and discovered that he was right. Margaret Ferris was indeed impressed with what he had done that morning.

CHAPTER

Oh, are you still here?" Chance had just come awake and saw young Ike Hadley pulling on his boots on the other side of camp. The insult was the first thing that came to his mind, for he still had a sour feeling about the Hadley boy. He had known as soon as the lad had mouthed off last night that he was no more than a lousy Hadley, and the whole lot of them ran to nothing but bad. Carny and Wilson were nothing more than loudmouth drunken bullies for the most part. The fact that they had actually done a couple of good deeds in town of late didn't make any difference to Chance at all. How could you take a liking to someone who had spent their lifetime seeing how much trouble they could cause? It just wasn't humanly possible to his way of thinking. He shook his head in disbelief as he glanced across the camp in the dim morning light, knowing in his heart and mind that Ike Hadley didn't belong on this trek.

"Yeah, I'm still here," was the boy's reply. "Surprised, are you?"

"Now just settle down, boys," Dallas said, walking into camp with an armful of wood for the fire. "The day ain't old enough to start fighting yet. Hell, I ain't even had my coffee."

Chance pulled on his boots and plunked his John B. on his head while Dallas got a fire going. When he had risen to his full height and adjusted his gun belt, Chance still didn't seem to have any better disposition, about the day or anything else. "Just feed the kid and send him on his way, Dallas," he grumbled. "He's got no business being with us."

Dallas Bodeen pushed his hat back on his head and scratched his near gray hair in thought. His face wrinkled up in a frown and he squinted, as though looking off in the distance, and he said, "I don't know, Chance. I been giving that some thought and it 'pears to me we can use all the guns we can get. You recall what I told you 'bout them Injun tribes and all down where we're going, don't you?"

"Sure, but—"

"Made a life of studying Indians and their ways, I have," Dallas said in a prideful way to Manuel, as though to start a conversation or impart an important piece of knowledge. "Why, if they's west of the Big Muddy, I likely know the tribe from somewheres."

"Then you are a man of wisdom, *mi amigo,* and that is something to behold," Manuel said with only half a smile.

"I hope to tell you," was Dallas's somewhat forlorn reply. Then, nodding toward Chance and Ike, he added, "I just can't get young pups like these to listen to me. Manuel, it's purely strange how these young 'uns don't pick up their hearing until they get 'em a few gray hairs on they scalp."

The Mexican smiled from ear to ear, knowing exactly what the old mountain man was getting at. *"Sí. Es verdad."*

"I'm telling you, Dallas, he ain't nothing but a Hadley hothead," Chance said in a persistent manner. "He's gonna be nothing but trouble and I've got enough of that to worry about now. Adding to my problems ain't gonna make me no easier to get along with."

Dallas looked at Chance as though he were stark, raving mad. "Now, Chance, when in the hell have you ever been easy to get along with? Will you tell me that?"

"Damn it, you know what I mean, Dallas." Admitting to any of his shortcomings was not one of Chance Carston's more eloquent lines of speech. In fact, there didn't seem to be an awful lot that was eloquent about the older Carston brother or his speech.

"I think you're wrong about this Hadley, Chance. Why, the lad acted real respectful last night. And the only time he come close to flaring up was when you pushed him into it. Hell, I seen you get riled with less pushing than he took." Without waiting for another comment from Chance, Dallas turned to Ike. "Can you shoot worth a tinker's damn, son?"

Ike Hadley gave a modest shrug of the shoulder. "I generally hit what I aim at."

But Chance wasn't satisfied. "That ain't good enough. I need someone who's gonna hit *everything* they aim at."

"Señors, the food will burn and the coffee will boil

away if you continue to argue this way," Manuel said. "And it is still a good ride to my family's home."

Temporarily, the argument was set aside in favor of a cup of coffee and more biscuits and bacon. It was nothing like they might have been served at the Porter Café or the Ferris House, but it filled the void in their stomachs and gave them nourishment enough to want to get on with the day.

"Tell you what, Chance, you and Manuel stick to what's in front of us and where we're going, since you fellas know the way best," Dallas said when they were breaking camp. "Me and old Ike here—we'll watch the other three sides and let you know when we got visitors, especially the unwanted type." The old mountain man reached over and gave Ike Hadley a hearty slap on the back as though to convey friendship of a sort. Both his words and his actions surprised the seventeen-year-old.

Chance saw that he was arguing with someone who could be just as hardheaded as he at times and gave in to Dallas's wishes. Besides, the day was too short to spend it arguing over something—or somebody—that wasn't worth it. And Ike Hadley was far from worth it. "You gonna be responsible for him, then?" he asked Dallas as he nodded toward Ike.

"Why, sure. I doubt he'll give me so much as an ounce of trouble," was Dallas's reply.

"Then let's get the hell outta here," Chance said, looking across the Rio Grande to the vast country known as Mexico. "We're burning daylight."

"Thanks, Mr. Bodeen," a grateful Ike said as he saddled his mount and readied to ride. "I'll make you proud of me, I swear I will."

"You know, son, I got a notion it ain't me you're wanting to make feel busting with pride so much as it is that lunkhead brother of yours," Dallas said with raised eyebrow. "By the way, why don't you call me Dallas. That mister stuff is for my daddy and he's long been dead."

"Thank you, sir. I mean Dallas."

Dallas gave the boy a friendly wink and a nod as they made their way south into Mexico, riding behind Chance and Manuel.

The farther south you go into Mexico, the drier it gets, but that is to be expected. The water holes are farther and farther apart and smaller and smaller in size. It soon becomes imperative that you know what direction to head in if you wish to survive. Chance could scarcely remember what water holes he and Pa and Wash had stopped at on the way down four years back, but he had every confidence that Manuel would be able to lead them to the right spots as they made their way toward José and Rosa and their home. In a way he was glad that he could count on Manuel for at least that, for Chance Carston had other things on his mind.

Normally, Chance found sleep an easy and restorative thing, a part of the cycle of life that was needed to get on with it. But last night he had not gotten to sleep until close to midnight. It wasn't the ultimate confrontation with those who were threatening Manuel and his family that had bothered him, for he knew that when the time came he would function as he always did and do his damnedest to make sure that justice prevailed. It was what he had learned as a young Texas Ranger, and it was what had stuck with him all of these years, even if he no longer wore the badge.

What had bothered him was the concern Rachel had shown toward him and this adventure he was mbarking on. Perhaps *concern* wasn't the right word; erhaps *worry* was closer to correct. Of all the times he ad gone out, she had picked this time to tell him how nuch she felt about those dangerous situations.

No wonder Wash was feeling half crazed from the vorry Sarah Ann felt when he went out of late. Why, it vas enough to make a man forget what it was he was upposed to be doing, and that had happened once lready with Wash, back on that cattle drive with harlie Goodnight. Granted it was once, but it was nce too many, for Wash could have gotten them all illed if he had kept it up. Rachel should never have alked to him the way she did. He had found it had veighed heavy on his mind last night and was still eavy on his mind this morning. Only the argument vith Ike Hadley had brought him back to his senses nd the edge he normally felt on a trek like this. He early felt like thanking the boy for being there, but vasn't about to let him start to feel as sappy toward im as Ike had apparently begun to feel toward allas.

Water holes and campsites weren't the only thing a ody had to worry about once he crossed the Rio rande. There were the *federales.* For the most part ey did their job, which was patrolling the northern lexico border and keeping all unwanted visitors out f the country. Chance knew that the definition of *nwanted* could be broad, all depending on who was charge of the *federales* you encountered. If they ad spent the day chasing—or being chased by— enegade Indians, they might simply overlook your resence in their country and warn you to look out for e troublemakers they had been dealing with. On the ther hand, there were those who acted more like ounty hunters than border guards, and they were to be dealt with cautiously too. Troublemakers themselves, they were often hired guns who wore the uniforms of *federales* they had killed and were now masquerading as them. They would sign on with a local cattle rustler or horse thief, approach you in a peaceful manner, then shoot you in the back when you passed them by. Naturally, they were only after your horses, weapons, and supplies. The dead bodies they left for the buzzards.

The morning passed quietly and they were about to stop at a water hole and give the horses and themselves a break when Chance heard the sound of approaching horses. He looked to his left, at Manuel. "If they ain't friendly, you make damn sure that Sharps of yours hits its mark, amigo," he said, a frown already forming on his forehead. Something told him this country was just as unfriendly and inhospitable as the last time he had been in it. Over his shoulder he saw Dallas whisper something to Ike Hadley. When he was through palavering, Dallas and Ike both moved their horses and themselves away from Chance and Manuel, situating themselves about twenty feet out to the side of them and facing them at an angle. Chance knew the move was designed to make whomever their visitors were a mite uncomfortable.

At first glance Chance didn't think there could be more than half a dozen of them, maybe five at the most. One thing was for sure—they didn't make any secret of heading toward them. The closer they got the more Chance could see the gaudy apparel they wore on their saddles. Leave it to a Mexican to get flamboyant with his saddle doodads. Only one of them had on the uniform of a *federale*.

They came in at an easy lope, riding as though getting to the water hole was the least of their worries.

'They carry *muchas pistolas.* They are heavily ırmed," Manuel said. Chance thought he heard a hint ıf fear in the man's words and it bothered him.

"That they are, Manuel," he replied in a calm tone. 'Even got 'em a couple of rifles, I see." He spoke as hough he were making idle conversation, hoping his ıwn words would spark some bravery in the man ıeside him.

There turned out to be five of them, and they rode ıp to Chance and his friends as bold as brass. A crawny one and his friend seemed to be the talkers in he outfit.

"It is a hot day, amigo, no?" the scrawny one said vith a smile that exposed crooked and slightly blackned teeth. It was he who, except for his headgear, vore the uniform of a *federale.* He took off his ombrero with one hand and wiped the sleeve of that and across his forehead, taking away some sweat vith it.

"It's a hot day, yes," Chance said in an even voice. Might get hotter before the afternoon is out." Will nd Wash Carston had heard words like this before om Chance. They were the kind of words that only hance would come up with. But then, they were the ind of words that were an invitation to a shooting ıatch and only Chance didn't seem to fear them. fter a moment of silence, Chance said, "There seems ı be water aplenty for all of us and the horses. Unless, f course, you want to fight over it."

The scrawny one suddenly lost his smile, replacing with a rather ugly and frustrated look. "Señor, do ɔu know where you are?"

Chance made up his mind then and there that this ıan had absolutely nothing to do with the *federales* ıd that he was nothing more than a hired gun of some kind. With a great deal of deliberateness he dismounted, swatting his horse on the butt and sending it out of the line of fire he knew would be forthcoming.

"Looks to me to be a water hole with a whole lot of open space around it," he said, planting his hands on his hips and smiling back at the scrawny one, just to let him know he had the better of him.

"You are on the land of the cousin of Juan Cortinas, señor."

Chance's smile widened. "Are you bragging or complaining?" Like most who had heard the legend spread about him, Chance knew that Juan Cortinas was some sort of Mexican *bandido* who specialized in raiding both sides of the Rio Grande and stealing cattle and horses, then selling them to comancheros and others who made their living south of the border in Mexico.

"Do you not know who Juan Cortinas is?" Scrawny asked in surprise at Chance's apparent ignorance.

"Sure do." Chance nodded. "Fact is, I'm real disappointed he ain't here to speak for himself. I got a notion he's a whole lot scarier than you are, amigo."

The fat one started palavering away in Spanish, spouting off about something to the scrawny one. Chance didn't even bother to ask Manuel what they were talking about.

"Let me ask you something, amigo," Chance said.

"Señor?"

"Do you know where *you* are?"

Scrawny was now confused and mad.

"Only reason I ask is a body ought to know where it is he's gonna die. Don't you think?" Another moment's pause and Chance added, "That is what you rode up to us for, ain't it?"

If Chance were to be accused of pushing for a fight, e would likely have to admit to being guilty to it, but e also knew that the hombres before him would hoot him in the back as soon as he had his back urned to them and he'd just as soon get it over with ere and now. He just wanted one of them to go for his un first.

The one on his right and Scrawny seemed to think like for both reached for their six-guns at once. hance had his out before Scrawny could even clear eather and shot him high in the chest, knocking him ff his horse. His gun went off wild as he fell to the round. By the time the troublemaker had come close o regaining his balance, Chance had plugged him a econd time, sure the man was dead as he fell back to he ground.

The others of Scrawny's friends, although they ight have been good with a six-gun, were either not nat accurate or not that fast. But then, not everyone ith Chance was either. Manuel had nervously rought his Sharps rifle down on the fat one, only to re too quickly and shoot the man's horse square etween the eyes instead of shooting the man. Chance ad to shoot him twice, too, to make sure he was dead. le was.

Dallas had done little more than bring his Henry fle down on his hip and fire at the man on the far left. le hit him high in the side, the bullet traveling rough the body until it punctured the man's heart nd he fell from his horse, dead. But then, Dallas had een around for upwards of seventy years and had arned a number of ways of surviving during those any years.

It was Ike Hadley who seemed to have some trouble oing his target in. First off, he found out he wasn't as fast as he thought he was, for his opponent—the man on the far right who had drawn his six-gun at the same time as Scrawny—shot Ike's hat off before Ike could shoot him. And when he shot him he only hit him in the leg. Ike never was sure if it was the loud sound of his six-gun or what, but the man apparently didn't like being shot and turned tail and beat a path away from them. With him was the man next to him, who also spurred his horse until it was riding fast as the wind in the opposite direction. Ike wound up firing three more rounds at the pair who were in retreat but did no damage that he could tell.

"Didn't them brothers of yours ever teach you anything, sonny?" Chance asked angrily.

"Like what?" Ike said, still trying to gain control of his mount, who had been skittish ever since the shooting started.

"Don't never do no shooting fight from the top of your saddle unless you have to," Chance said as he grabbed the reins of Ike's horse and calmed it down. "Most folks can't shoot worth a damn atop a horse. You just proved that."

"But I hit him!" Ike seemed determined to prove that he had done something right for a change.

"May be, kid, but you hit him in the wrong place. Unless you hit him in the chest or the face, your shooting ain't been worth spit. Oh, you hit him in the leg and you scared him off all right, but I'd bet a dollar that scrawny son of a bitch has got him a boss not far off. And once they find out what happened to their hired hands, why, they'll be hunting us up in real quick fashion."

Ike Hadley was more frustrated than mad as he dismounted his horse and began to reload his six-gun. And he didn't seem fearful at all when he looked over at Chance, a scowl on his own face as he said, "Dallas is right. Ain't nobody ever gonna please you. Not even the devil himself, I'd say."

When Chance gave a hard look at the old mountain man, Dallas only grinned back at him, for he knew Ike was right.

CHAPTER

They weren't at the water hole more than half an hour if you counted from the time the hired guns rode up to the time they had eaten a small bite, watered their horses, and continued their ride south. What took up most of their time was stripping the scrawny one and his *compadres* of their weapons and ammunition and what little food they had in their saddlebags. Chance had no second thoughts about stripping the dead while Ike Hadley seemed a mite squeamish about the whole ordeal.

"Can't bring yourself to do it, that the problem Hadley?" Chance said, kneeling down beside Scrawny and emptying his pockets after he relieved him of his six-guns, ammunition, and knife. Ike only stood there with a queasy look on his face, as though he found the whole act repulsive.

"It just don't seem right," was all he could think to say. "Even taking their money?" he added when he saw Chance deposit several coins he had found in Scrawny's pockets into the pocket of his own denim jeans.

"He sure ain't gonna need it where he's going," Chance said, not missing a beat as he continued to strip the man of his possessions. "And he sure ain't among the living."

"Chance is right," Manuel said, his own arms loaded with several rifles and bandoleers of ammunition he had liberated from the gunmen's saddles. "Men like this—they have no relatives to forward their life savings to, as meager as it is." He looked down at Scrawny and chuckled to himself. "As ugly as this one is, his *madre* must have thrown him out with the dishwater, and done it on purpose."

Dallas gave the young man a friendly slap on the back. "Riding into the jaws of hell and handing those coins over to Beelzebub himself is as close as you're likely to come to a family for that yahoo," he said with a nod. "And I don't know about you, Ike, but I've no intention of visiting hell any sooner than I'm called to."

"You just mind what I said. They'll catch up with us soon enough and then we'll all get a dose of hell." Those were Chance's last words on the subject.

They took the two extra horses with them, leaving the one Manuel had killed and the bodies of the dead men. "They deserve it," Chance had commented as they left the water hole. "Likely kill off a whole bunch of buzzards."

Their ride the rest of the afternoon was relatively peaceful, perhaps because they seemed to be the only ones foolish enough to be out in the blistering heat. Or was it the two extra horses, now laden with rifles, pistols, and two sawed-off shotguns, that were slowing them down? Whether it be heat, horses, or a combination of both, none of them felt as though they had traveled as far as they should have that day. Particularly Manuel, who among all of them had an overriding interest in getting back to José, Rosa, and the children. Yet his side and his bones were still healing and toward the end of the day, when they came on another water hole, he was blaming himself for their lack of speed.

"How badly did I do today?" he asked Chance when Dallas and Ike were making the evening meal and the horses were settled in.

But Chance was all too well aware of the mistake Manuel had made during the shoot-out, and although he truly felt like letting the Mexican know what shoddy work he thought it was, he did not. It had been hard not to spot the sour look that had developed on Manuel's face late that afternoon, hard not to see the man was displeased with himself about something.

"Don't worry about it, pard," Chance said in an understanding tone. "Mistakes happen."

Ike looked up across the fire, his face suddenly filled with anger. "How come when he steps in horse apples it's a mistake, but when I do it, it stinks to high heaven?" he asked in what Chance thought to be a growl.

"In case you didn't know, pilgrim, Manuel here got pretty busted up riding to get me," Chance growled back. "I figure he was lucky to get off a shot in that fuss back there. Besides," he added after a moment's pause, "he's got plenty of other things on his mind. It's his family we're gonna be pulling out of a fix, you know."

Chance's words only brought out more anger in the young Hadley, and Ike said, "What about me? I got a brother back there I don't even know is dead or alive. Hell, I got things on my mind, too, damn it."

"Don't be smart, kid." If the look on him was any indication, Chance was about ready to jump across the campfire and beat the living daylights out of young Hadley. "You're the one who wanted to come along and be some kind of hero. I damn sure didn't ask you. Hell, I ain't seen much in the line of heroics, as far as hat goes," he said as an afterthought.

"Why is it every time we stop for a decent meal you wo want to go at one another's throats?" Dallas nterrupted, sounding like a parent addressing wo annoying children. It was plain to see that Ike vanted to fight Chance but had the good sense—or ack of guts, one or the other—to keep his mouth hut. At least for now. As for Chance, Dallas had een him fight at the drop of a hat and figured the angy Carston was simply waiting for someone to drop a hat. "Now stop the nonsense before these Mexican strawberries and the coffee both boil over," e added, and began to dish out part of the evening meal.

Chance was still flat-out angry when he took his late and cup, but Ike had turned sullen and left the amp area, headed for the horses from the looks of im. Dallas felt a bit of relief when he saw that, nowing it would do both Chance and Ike good to be way from one another until they cooled down. It was Manuel who seemed to feel guilty about the whole ning.

"I am sure that the boy is much braver than I," he said around a mouthful of beans.

"I wouldn't give him credit for spit, Manuel. He ain't done nothing yet to impress me," Chance said his tone still angry.

"You might watch words like that, Chance," Dallas said. "I got a notion someday you may eat 'em. That boy ever finds himself, he's gonna show whoever's around him that he's just full of surprises. But I'll tell you one thing, Chance, you treating him like so much cow pie—why, that ain't gonna do him no good at all."

"I think Dallas is right, Señor Chance. Like the toreador, he will be *muy bravo* when he fights the bull," Manuel said in a humble way. When no one commented on his words, he added, "I meant what I said about Señor Ike, for I am not brave at all." He then proceeded to tell Chance and Dallas how he had hidden from the plug uglies who had ridden up to the house and beaten José. He was particularly ashamed of not stepping out and helping his family, weapon or no weapon.

Chance set down his empty plate, his coffee cup still in hand. He now thought he knew what it was that had been eating away at the Mexican all afternoon, what it was that had made him so angry with himself by the time they made camp. "Don't sell yourself short, amigo. Pa always said sometimes it was better to pull your freight than pull your gun."

"That's a fact, Manuel," Dallas added. "Why, an' you run out there and surprised 'em, the whole pack of them fools might have decided to kill you all on the spot. You done just fine." Dallas took a sip of coffee then smiled to himself. "Besides, I'd never have had the chance to get down into Mexico. Only south-of

he-border Mexico I been to was thirty some years
ack and that was around the Taos and Santa Fe area.
Mostly mountains, you know."

Chance and Manuel had been so taken by the old
nountain man's words that they didn't hear the men
pproach their camp. One of them stepped around a
ottonwood they had camped near. He had drawn his
un, apparently as a matter of precaution. He was also
ressed in the uniform of a *federale,* which immedi-
tely gave Chance and Dallas cause for alarm.

"No, señor, that will not be necessary," the man
aid when he saw Chance reaching for his six-gun.
'My men and I are not here to harm you." At this
ime two more men dressed in uniforms appeared
rom some brush next to the cottonwood. "We must
imply ask you some questions. For example, what it
s that you *norteamericanos* are doing here?"

Manuel seemed to take over from there and the two
nen talked back and forth for several minutes in their
ative tongue. Some of it Chance and Dallas picked
p, but not all of it. When they were through, Chance
ad the notion that they both understood one an-
ther.

"I have explained to him that you are a breaker of
orses and a longtime friend of mine," Manuel told
hance, remembering what Chance did for a living
hen he wasn't out chasing outlaws and killers. It was
e horses, after all, that had brought the Carston
amily to his abode in the first place. To Dallas he said,
You are my expert hunter and tracker."

The old mountain man's chest swelled up at the
ords. "Well, now, it's been a few years since I was
escribed with words that were that . . . expert, to
oin a phrase."

Manuel laughed to himself. "The *federale,* a Captain García-Ramirez, assures me that he is who he says he is. I believe him. I briefly told him of our encounter with the others this morning. He has heard of them. They are trouble and he hunts for them."

"Maybe I can finish my coffee now," Chance said with a sigh of relief.

Then they all had a surprise.

"You know, I could kill you real easy from right here." It was the voice of Ike Hadley and he stood behind a clump of bushes on the far side of the camp, apparently out of sight of the captain and his men. But now he stood at his full height, nearly six feet tall, and held Carny Hadley's six-gun at full length. It was aimed directly at the captain's chest.

"Put the goddamn gun away, Hadley—he's on our side," Chance said, feeling a bit embarrassed at the foolish move the seventeen-year-old had made. When Hadley could only muster a confused look, he yelled, "Put the gun away, damn it!" This brought Ike Hadley back to reality and he quickly holstered his six-gun.

"He's young," Dallas said, obviously put off by Ike's actions.

Chance glanced at Manuel and said, "Tell the captain we also have an idiot in camp."

"You do not give me much credit, señors," the captain said. Without waiting for a reply, he looked out past the camp and yelled, "Pedro!" A rustle was made in the brush and another *federale* now stood up in plain view. At port arms he held a rather old musket, but it was evident that he knew how to use it and would have killed Ike Hadley or anyone else who had made a move to harm his captain.

"I reckon we underestimated you, Captain," Dallas said. "That we did."

Manuel made much in the way of apology to the captain and his men and shortly the *federales* were gone.

Ike Hadley, for all his trying, still hadn't shown Chance much in the way of heroics.

CHAPTER

★ 11 ★

It was the next morning that Harry Aker and Sam Bayles almost tipped their hand.

Ever since he'd gone, Rachel Ferris had been getting more and more worried over whether Chance would be coming back. It had only been a few days but she had become noticeably preoccupied with the man she was falling in love with. Margaret had noticed her daughter's prepossession and made a mental note to talk to her about it, but it was already too late. Rachel left the kitchen with a tray full of plates and proceeded to slide a pair of sunny-side-up eggs right into Harry Aker's lap before setting the plate down on the community table.

"Ouch!" Harry had cried out, as a hot slice of ham slid after the eggs onto his lap. This was followed by

"Damn it!" as he quickly stood up and brushed the food off his denim pants. "What kind of service do you call that?" the irate customer bellowed.

Sam Bayles was quicker of mind than his partner and picked up on the fact that Will Carston was also seated at the table. The last thing they needed was some kind of trouble with the local law, so he reached up and grabbed his partner by the arm, pulling him down into his seat, saying, "Sit down, Harry. It's just an honest mistake. No harm done."

Wilson Hadley was seated on the other side of Harry Aker and had immediately noticed the man's loud mouth. He and Carny had helped out the Ferris women in the past and Wilson, for one, had grown fond of the mother-and-daughter team. As far as he was concerned, they did a whale of a job running the boardinghouse and serving three damn-good meals a day. Hell, it was more than most men could manage—more than he could manage of that rundown place he and his brothers were living in. In his wildest dreams he occasionally thought of asking one of the Ferris women to cook for him on a part-time basis but knew it would never happen. First off, neither Margaret nor Rachel would consent to it. They had too much to do here at the boardinghouse. Second, and perhaps most important, neither Will nor Chance Carston would ever permit Margaret and Rachel to do such a thing. Strong minded as those women were (it was common knowledge that Will was sweet on Margaret and Rachel had set her cap for Chance Carston), there were just certain things they wouldn't do, and catering to the Hadley brothers was one of them, Wilson thought.

"I'd listen to what your pard says, friend. It never does pay to run your mouth at a woman in a strange

town." Picking up the knife he'd used to cut his mea
with, he twisted it around some, gazing back and fortl
between it and the man he was talking to. "Never car
tell what'll happen."

"I think he gets the point, Mr. Hadley," Margare
said as she appeared on the scene. As soon as Rache
had spilled the plate of eggs, she had burst into tear
and abandoned her tray of food, heading for the safet
of the kitchen.

It was obvious to all at the table that Harry Ake
was madder than a wet hen and desperately wanted t
take it out on someone, preferably the person who ha
done this to him. But Sam Bayles was doing a
admirable job of holding his partner in place with on
hand—firmly placed at the elbow—and wolfing dow
his plate of ham and scrambled eggs with the other
His partner might not get his breakfast meal but h
damn sure was going to eat his. By the time Margare
had appeared and commented on Wilson Hadley'
knife twisting, he was done with his food.

"Oh, please, no payment is necessary," Margare
had said when he'd risen from the community tabl
and begun to dig in his pocket for a coin. "After all, i
was our fault. I'll cook up some more eggs for yo
right away."

"Thank you, ma'am, I appreciate it," he said ner
vously. He couldn't wait to get out of there. With
weak grin he added, "But I reckon my partner needs
bath anyways."

They made an odd couple as they left the boarding
house, Sam Bayles seemingly embarrassed for wha
had happened to his friend, while Harry Aker looke
as though he could kill someone if he were given th
chance.

"Couple of odd birds, if you ask me," Will Carston said as he watched them go.

"Yes, they are indeed, my good man," Jeremiah Younger said in agreement. He didn't say anything to the lawman next to him, but he fully expected to check out the two men known as Harry Aker and Sam Bayles. "I'll be along with your brother's meal within the hour, Mr. Hadley," he added as Wilson Hadley tossed a coin next to his plate, got up, and left the Ferris House.

"Thanks, tinhorn," the big man said in his raspy voice, not even bothering to look over his shoulder as he spoke. The man's words set the gambler to wondering about Wilson Hadley as well as Aker and Bayles.

He voluntarily began to clean up the mess left behind by Harry Aker. When he took the scraps of food into the kitchen, he found Rachel Ferris standing there, still bawling her eyes out. He knew that her mother would talk to her later about what it was that was bothering her, but he also knew from experience that the pain a person feels immediately after a failure is some of the worst that can be undergone. What were needed then, he knew, were a confident word and a hug from a friend. And perhaps a good laugh over the whole situation.

"There, there, child," he said in almost a whisper, setting his plate of scraps down on a nearby table and placing an arm around her shoulders. "It isn't all that bad now, is it? After all, the only thing you forgot to give him was more coffee."

The crying soon ceased and Rachel looked up at the tall, gangly gambler, who was now smiling down at her as though she were his prize pupil and he were offering an encouraging word after she had just fallen short of winning the spelling bee. One thing Jeremiah Younger had been told over the years was that he had an engaging smile and that it was sometimes even contagious. At present it seemed to be, as Rachel smiled back at him. Wiping her hanky across her sniffling nose, she said, "You know, you're funny, Mr. Younger. I bet Sarah Ann would like to hear that," she added, and proceeded to tell him about the time Sarah Ann Carston (née Porter) had poured a pot of coffee into Wilson Hadley's lap when he'd started making trouble.

"And I'll bet he's on his best manners in that establishment now, isn't he?" Jeremiah smiled.

Rachel nodded. "Why is it you older men know so much?" she asked out of the blue. He still had his hand around her shoulder and she hadn't asked him to remove it or tried to shrug it off. Truth to tell, it felt sort of comfortable to Jeremiah Younger.

"Honestly, my dear, it is a condition of age more than knowledge," he chuckled. "If one desires to live long in this world, one picks it up at a moment's notice over the years."

As soon as Rachel's smile had appeared, it vanished, replaced by a sad look.

"Ah, now we come to the true reason for your outflow of tears," he said, the smile only slightly evident on his face, for he knew that no matter what he might think, the subject matter he was now approaching was quite heavy on this young lady's heart and mind.

"Yes, I'm afraid so." Still a sad, melancholy look.

"And if I had a dollar, I would bet it was an affair of the heart," Younger added.

Rachel blushed guiltily. "You'd win a dollar." At first she was reluctant to tell him of her worries, of her loves. After all, even though he'd been in town little over a week and seemed to be a charming man on all counts, he was nevertheless a stranger to her. Still, maybe an outsider would be able to give her some fresh insight into this turmoil she was putting herself through—that Chance was putting her through. So bit by bit Rachel explained the consternation she was feeling over Chance and this adventure he had gone on. "What do you think?" she asked when she was through pouring out her story. "Am I really worrying over nothing?"

Jeremiah Younger rubbed his hand across his thoughtful face for a moment before saying, "Chance, you say his moniker is? Rather a tall, husky fellow, a bit dark in complexion as well as mood on occasion?"

"Yes, that would be Chance. Why, have you met him?"

The pleasant smile appeared once again. "As a matter of fact, I have, my dear. In the saloon the other day. Nothing more than a cordial passing of words." One thing Jeremiah Younger knew was that he wasn't about to go into detail as to what those words were, for they could prove more than embarrassing to him.

"He's quite a man, isn't he?" Rachel said. Younger noticed that at mention of her beau's name this young lady became quite proud.

"Yes, indeed, he is, my dear." Younger meant every word of it, for he had been quite impressed with Chance Carston's words, although he wasn't about to admit that it was Chance's words *and* actions that had driven him to his own depths of despair.

He turned Rachel so she faced him, then placed a hand on each dainty shoulder and held her at arm's length from him. With a confident smile, one he hadn't felt or expressed in a long time, he said, "My dear, you must listen to this *old man's* words. I saw a great deal of strength in your beau that one time I did meet him. I have no fear that he will not return from his mission, whatever that may be. And neither should you."

Rachel blushed deeper when Jeremiah Younger bent down and lightly kissed her on the forehead, smiled and winked at her, and concluded their conversation with, "Now then, where is that Hadley fellow's meal?"

CHAPTER

★ 12 ★

From the time they awoke until they broke camp the ext morning, all Chance could do was glare at Ike Hadley with an intensity that Dallas was sure bor-ered on pure hatred. The old mountain man decided was healthier to have his conversations with the Iexican, for Ike wasn't looking any too pleased this iorning either. It was just that with Ike Hadley, why, ie boy was likely mad at himself more than he ever ould be at Chance Carston. Young 'uns like that nded to get that way. But then, how are you sup-osed to feel when you damn near get everyone in amp killed? Dallas knew he'd likely feel the same as e did now. In fact, there was that time way back hen . . .

"What do you think, Manuel?" Dallas asked as he and the Mexican were preparing breakfast over the fire. "Dueling pistols at twenty paces?" He was only half joshing about the matter when he spoke.

Manuel looked across camp, Chance sitting on a dead log on the east side, young Ike sitting by himself on the west side, and shook his head in uncertainty. "I don't know, señor. Were it up to me, I would take the *pistolas* away from the children before they hurt themselves," he said in dead seriousness. In a lighter tone, he glanced at Dallas and smiled, adding, "Or us."

"Know what you mean, amigo," the mountain man said, cracking a smile for the first time that morning. "Been pondering that my own self."

The air about camp didn't seem to improve, even after all four of them had had their fill of the morning meal. Chance and Ike were still as silent as the members of a Sunday prayer meeting, although the looks they exchanged were getting downright hostile. All Dallas could figure was Chance didn't like Ike for his half-assed attempt at getting them shot by the *federales* last night. And Ike, well, it appeared he was getting a mite perturbed at the constant threatening glares Chance was giving him.

"You say you figure it's the better part of a day's ride afore we get to your place, Manuel?" Dallas asked when they broke camp and mounted their horses.

"Sí, Dallas. By the time the sun sets we will be there," the Mexican replied. Dallas noticed that although he was able to climb in the saddle much more easily than the day before, Manuel still had a look of pain about him when he had to move around on his horse.

"Well, good. I just hope we run into the whole

goddamn Comanche nation before the day is out," Dallas said in a matter-of-fact way.

"Señor?" Manuel said with eyebrows raised in surprise. Who in God's name would make such a wish but a crazy man?

"Why sure!" Dallas looked over his shoulder at Chance and Ike, both still speechless, and snarled as he said, "I was hoping to sit by and watch these two *children* wipe out every Comanche brave in all of Texas and Mexico. At least, maybe they'll git whatever s in their systems out."

But Chance and Ike were both too proud to answer o Dallas's digs, and by the time they proceeded outh, the two of them were glaring at the old mounain man rather than at each other. Dallas didn't seem o care worth a whit.

The sun seemed to know they were on the trail for it hone bright and the day got hot within two hours of he time they had struck out. Dallas had been in esert country before and knew that once the greenery isappeared from the landscape there would be preious little water. It was midmorning when they topped to give their horses a rest and some water, aking a healthy amount for themselves as well. They ad just mounted up again when they heard a sound hat was both strange and familiar.

"Was that a whippoorwill?" Chance asked, speakng for the first time that day other than to ask for nore coffee at breakfast.

"You know, I think you're right," Dallas said, for is ears had perked up at the sound of the bird, too.

What transpired next was a bothersome look beveen Chance and Dallas. Both were well aware that a t of old-timers, especially Rangers, had used the call the whippoorwill to contact one another when they

were out of sight and maybe in a bit of a difficulty. I
was mostly a warning signal used by frontiersmen
And the reason the frontiersman used it was because
although there was indeed such a bird as the whip
poorwill, it was one found in the eastern contours o
the United States that seldom if ever made its wa
west of the Mississippi. Therefore, if a man heard it
he could be nearly certain that it was another whit
man who was initiating the call. But Chance an
Dallas weren't wondering who had initiated this cal
What they were both thinking right now was that i
was also possible for an Indian to learn and imitat
the call. Both men were soon scanning the horizon
looking for someone or something that wasn't sup
posed to be there.

In no time they found it.

"Oh, shit!" Dallas all but whispered as he spotted
group of riders suddenly appearing on the easter
horizon. His original suspicion was that they wer
comancheros, but he soon dispelled that though
Perhaps half of them were indeed comancheros, bu
by the look of them the other half were renegad
Indians. It was just that by the war paint they had or
why, they didn't look a damn thing like Comanches a
all. But they sure were armed!

"This way, amigos!" Manuel yelled before anyon
could get out another word. "The gully!" he added a
he beat his mount across the tail with his reins and le
them toward cover.

"Looks like you got your wish, Dallas," Chanc
yelled as he wheeled his horse to follow Manuel.

"Only partly, son," was Dallas's calm reply, he to
wheeling his horse to head for cover in the gull
"Them ain't Comanches."

The raiding party was still a hundred yards fro

them, but the two ex-Rangers soon had their horses at full gallop as they followed Ike and Manuel.

"What the hell are they then?" Chance yelled at the old mountain man as they rode side by side.

"Apaches!" Dallas yelled back.

Chance wasn't sure about Dallas but he'd had a run-in or two with the Apaches before. He didn't know why, but the first thing that came to his mind was the trouble they had had with the Apaches once he, Charlie Goodnight, and Wash had gotten that herd of cattle across the Staked Plain and the Pecos. Having to fight the damned heat had been bad enough, but when those Apaches had crept up on hem as soon as they crossed the Pecos, why, herding hose cattle became a real chore. The second thing hat crossed his mind was that there was something lightly different about the Apaches compared to the Comanches, but for the life of him, he couldn't put his inger on it. Damn, it made him mad!

By the time they reached the gully, shots had been red at them and an arrow or two was flying through he air. They still had the extra horses they had taken rom the gang of would-be outlaws they'd had a run-in ith; two of the spare mounts had arrows stuck in the addle by the time they had reached the ravine.

The only one who was slow dismounting was Manu-l. He might have died then and there if he had been ny slower, for an arrow flew right over his shoulder, he edge of it slightly cutting the back of his neck. But he wound was insignificant and didn't stop the Mexican from grabbing what Dallas would call a possibles bag" filled with ammunition for his old harps rifle and banging away at the charging Indians.

Chance had the Spencer rifle in his hand by the time is feet had landed on the ground, but he knew good and well he'd need more than the seven-shot rifle to do in his attackers. He was also used to being in charge of the situation and immediately started giving orders. But it was only Ike Hadley he was ordering around.

"Give me that Henry!" he growled, and grabbed the rifle from the Hadley boy's hand. "See that bundle of rifles?" he ordered next, nodding at the extra weapons he had taken from the men in that first shoot-out. Before Ike could nod, he continued, wasting not a word. "They oughtta be loaded. You start feeding 'em to us as we need 'em. And keep an eye on these horses." Before making his way back to the edge of the ravine and the charging Apaches, Chance could have dug a knife in Ike Hadley's stomach and twisted it with less effect than the words he spoke now. "You let the *real* men do the fighting here."

Dallas aimed at every rider who came into sight and knocked two Apaches off their horses before they got close enough to do any killing. It had been a while since he'd fought Apaches and he could only hope that their leader would be riding up front like most other tribes had their men do. With a little bit of luck maybe he could kill one of them and the band would cut and run. But it didn't seem like he was having any luck so far. By the time he had shot his wad with the Henry, the comancheros and Apaches were close enough for him to see the whites of their teeth and he found himself getting slightly worried over the situation.

Manuel's fire was slow but steady and for the most part he hit what he aimed at, killing both horses and riders. After the war party made several passes, one lone rider headed straight for them rather than veer his pony off to the side like the others did. Manuel was standing back down the slope, doing his best to reload

:he Sharps, when pony and rider came flying over the ɛdge of the ravine. He didn't know whether he could ɩit the rider or not, as poor a shot as he had been, so Manuel simply turned the Sharps on the horse and ;hot it dead in midair. The pony collapsed on hitting he ground, the Indian rider rolling free. But before he Apache could regain his footing, Manuel was upon ɩim, swinging the Sharps as if it were a club. The ɔarrel of the heavy rifle knocked the brave uncon-cious. Then, in two quick motions, Manuel smashed n the Apache's face, killing him where he lay.

Chance had fired fast and hard as the raiding party ıttacked. He did a fast job of emptying the Spencer ifle into the riders, killing two comancheros and vounding several Apaches, he thought. In another ɔass he had emptied a spare Henry rifle that Ike ıanded him. It was when they made their third pass at hem—when Manuel killed the Indian pony—that Chance suddenly remembered what it was that ɩarked the Apache as being different from the Co-ɩanche. And it almost cost him his life.

As pitifully sad as Ike Hadley felt upon hearing Chance's degrading remark, he also knew he had a job ɔ do. With one hand he tried to hold the horses' reins nd keep them as calm as possible, as though such a ɛat were possible with this much shooting going on. Vith the other hand he dispensed the extra rifles he'd nbundled, keeping Dallas, Chance, and Manuel ɛadily armed, as the need be. It seemed that each of ɩem required a newly loaded rifle each time the ɛnegades made another pass. And by the third pass ɛ had passed out the last of the loaded rifles. He was amned if he knew what they were going to do next, ɔr he had never been that fast a reloader, especially ith the new lever actions and their cartridges. It was when he glanced down the ravine and saw a handful of Apache warriors running toward Manuel and Chance that he knew he had to take a hand in this fight.

He quickly let go of the horses' reins and drew Carny's six-gun and fired once from the waist. He hit one of the braves in the stomach, he thought, for the brave stumbled and fell before trying to get to his feet again. With revolver held at arm's length, Ike fired three more shots into three more of the warriors. They, too, stumbled and fell as Ike walked forward, bold as you please, and planted each of his remaining shots, one each, into the fallen Indians.

It was when Chance heard the sound of Ike's six-gun to his rear that he remembered that the Apache liked to do his fighting more on his feet than the Comanche did. On his way back from that cattle drive, he had asked himself if the Apaches would have been as proficient with horses if they, too, had lived in Texas, like the Comanches. His rifle was empty now after firing its contents into what remained of the renegades, so he pulled his own Colt revolver and fired off two quick shots, killing two of the last braves who had snuck down the ravine to attack their flank. It almost surprised him that Ike Hadley had handled the situation as well as he did.

"Looks like they've had enough," Dallas said as he began to reload his Henry rifle. "They've skedaddled, it appears."

With the exception of Manuel, who had grabbed up a rifle still bearing ammunition and kept guard in case the hostiles hadn't left, the troops reloaded. They had been extremely lucky in that Manuel's minor cuts at the beginning of the fracas had been the only wound any of them had taken. However, two of the extra horses had taken bullets and arrows meant for them and lay in the gully dying. By the time the three had finished reloading, Manuel had decided that the dying horses had gone through enough pain and put a bullet n each one's head.

"Well, what do you think of Ike now, him saving your life and all?" Dallas, in a good mood, asked Chance. Coming out on top of a shoot-out always made him glad he was alive to tell the story.

But Chance had a frown of discontent on his face, particularly at the sound of Ike Hadley's name. "I say he's still a bad shot."

Dallas was taken aback. "How the hell can you say hat? Why, the lad saved your life."

"Hell, the kid had to shoot them three Indians twice each," Chance growled back at Dallas. "See them last wo that was coming down the ravine?" Chance pointed to the last fallen Apaches. "I done them in with one shot each."

"Oh. I see," Dallas said in a considerably humbler one. Ike and Manuel couldn't understand Chance's raggadocio and were too stunned to say much of nything.

"Got a problem with that?" Chance said. The uestions seemed directed more to Ike than anyone lse.

Ike said nothing, although by the look of him he amn sure wanted to.

"Here. Hold this," Dallas said, and stuck his Henry fle out, waiting for Chance to take it in his grasp. hen, when the big man did, he hauled off and hit him cross the jaw as hard as he could. If it had been on a at surface, Dallas would have knocked him ass over akettle, but as it was Chance only fell back into the de of the ravine. Dallas grabbed up his Henry before hance hit the dirt.

"Madre de Dios," Manuel muttered in astonishment.

Ike just stared at Chance sitting there in as much bewilderment as he felt.

Dallas wasn't stunned at all for he was the one now in control. "Damn it, Chance, I hope you get over acting like a jackass, 'cause I sure as hell am getting tired of your braying."

All three stared at the old mountain man, who was suddenly very dangerous.

"Well, come on, you fools! Let's find Manuel's home afore them bastards decide they want to use us for target practice again."

And so they prepared to go.

CHAPTER

★ 13 ★

As much as Dallas wanted to, they didn't leave right
way. The old mountain man had given Ike a hand
eloading all of their rifles, rebundling them, and tying
hem to the back of the lone extra horse they now had.
Manuel had stripped the two dead horses of what
sable gear they had—extra rifles, canteens, and
mmunition. But it was Chance who fell to what was
onsidered by most to be a vile and vicious act.
Manuel was the first to notice as Chance pulled out
he bowie knife he carried on the left side of his gun
elt and cut the topknot off one of the dead Apaches.
nce he had accomplished this, he stuffed the bloody
artial scalp into the warrior's mouth. It made a
uesome sight at best.

"Madre de Dios," Manuel said in a soft voice, filled

with both awe and disgust. "Must you do this? Why not bury them, like a civilized man would?"

"I'll make sure I put that on your grave marker Manuel," Chance said in a hard, even tone. " 'Here lies Manuel. He died a civilized man.' "

Dallas stepped in before Chance wound up getting into another fight. "What he's getting at, amigo, is these fools we been dealing with the past hour or so why, they ain't nothing close to what you or I know a being civilized."

"But—"

"Chance knows as well as I do that these Apaches will be back to pick up their dead, just like the Comanches will do. And when they do, they'll see these heathens and know that they're dealing with some fellas who can play their own deadly game."

"Then you are inviting revenge," Manuel said. "Are you not inviting them to hunt you down because o your perversion to their kin?"

Chance shrugged, not caring one way or another "Could be, Manuel, but I'll tell you something." He had developed a deep frown as he spoke and his voice had dropped an octave, pure hatred in it now as he added, "We're in their territory now, and I've a notion they'd come after us one way or another. Besides, in case you didn't notice it, I spotted some comanchero amongst that group of riders. They look almighty similar to the ones you was describing to me back in Twin Rifles. That being the situation, well, like I say they'll know who they're dealing with now."

And that was that as Chance made the rest of the si who had been killed in the ravine look exactly like the first one he had done his work on.

Finally, they saddled up and continued their journey.

The silence they rode in the rest of the day was murderous at best. All four of them had gotten angry nough to kill anyone who might get in their way now, specially Chance and Ike. Chance had never gotten ised to being laid out on the ground like Dallas Bodeen had just done to him. And Ike Hadley, well, ie was downright put off by the ingratitude that had een shown him by Chance at having saved his life. Why, even the Mexican had mumbled a humble "*Gracias*" when they had mounted up again. He was iguring that the next time such an event occurred, he vould let the damned Indians cut and shoot Chance Carston all they wanted. Hell, the man likely had ice vater in his veins anyway.

As much pain as he was in, Manuel quickened the ace of his horse in hopes of reaching José and Rosa efore sundown. The sun beat down on them with a erceness that only a Gila monster could appreciate hat afternoon. If nothing else, both man and horse vere glad to stop at the one water hole they came cross that afternoon.

There was about an hour's worth of daylight left vhen they came over the rise and Chance recognized ie adobe structure he knew as belonging to José and osa Quesada. Both rider and horse were tired from ie prolonged heat of the day. But the horses smelled ie water in the waiting trough and broke into a gentle pe as they headed down the rise toward the adobe ouse. None of them saw anyone outside in the yard r curiously looking from behind the cloth curtains of ie windows. Nor were the children in sight.

Dallas had a cautious look about him as he reined his horse. But it was Chance, the deep frown still rominent on his forehead, who acted as though he ad never left the home of the Quesadas. As he did with all events in life, he encountered this one head-on. In this case he simply opened the door without even announcing himself.

And almost got himself killed.

If he thought he would be met with open arms, he was deathly wrong. As he pushed the door open, the first and only thing he saw was Rosa standing a good dozen feet away from him. She looked scared to death and desperate, to say the least. It was reflex action that made Chance go for his Colt revolver and yank it halfway out of its holster when he saw the big bore of the Sharps buffalo rifle Rosa held firmly in her hands. The only thing that kept him from pulling his six-gun all the way out and using it was the fact that he recognized Rosa and the Sharps she had trained on him. Chance had been around long enough to know that your friends don't shoot you; of course, he also knew that a woman looking as scared as Rosa Quesada did just now was also likely to pull the trigger whether you were friend or foe.

"Sorry to be busting in on you like this, Rosa," he said in as soft a voice as he could muster. "It's me, Chance Carston, remember?" he added, reaffirming what he hoped was still a bond of friendship. That was about when Manuel came in and took the rifle away from Rosa. While Chance wiped a good deal of sweat from his forehead—not a bit of it was from the afternoon heat, either—Manuel and Rosa chattered back and forth in Spanish.

"I hope we are not too late, Señor Chance," Manuel said in a worried tone.

"How's that?"

"The big one, the *norteamericano,* was here again while we were gone. He has beaten José again," he said.

"How bad is he?" Chance asked Rosa, concern in is own voice.

Rosa pointed to the back corner of the house. hance's eyes were almost adjusted to the darkness nside and he thought he saw a man, José, lying there n a bed. "He wants to get out of bed but cannot. I tell im to stay in bed, but he is as stubborn as a goat."

Three quick strides and Chance was at the old nan's side. His face was black and blue on both heeks, even through the white of his beard, the emains of what was surely a welt on the side of his ead showing prominently. "I came as soon as Manel got the word to me, amigo." Trying to sound ositive, which was not at all how he actually felt, he miled, adding, "Saddled my best horse, rounded up a w friends of mine who wanted to take 'em a ride, nd blazed a trail getting here. That I did, José."

Jose slowly reached a hand up and took hold of hance's big hamlike fist. "You will pardon me if I do ot rise," he said, and smiled through all his pain.

"Hell, I ain't never been formal, you know that," hance said, returning the smile. Apparently, both en felt ill at ease about this meeting.

"There are too many bruises. Too many bruises." ith the same slow movement he had used to shake hance's hand, José moved the other hand to his est and rubbed it in circles. "I fear the bones are oken or I would go to the fight with you." Then his ice faded and he began to cough in spasms, spitting a pan on the floor.

"Had me a few of them busted bones, too," Chance id with a nod. "Know how you feel. Bothersome as n be."

José smiled. *"Sí."*

Dallas approached the two, his Henry rifle seated

firmly in the crook of his arm. "Well, now, you loo
like a man I could have a decent conversation with,'
he said to José as he introduced himself.

José smiled again. "I would like that sometime."

"Don't blame you for wanting to get up and mov
about," Dallas said to the bedridden man. To Chance
he said, "Seems we're dealing with more than just
handful of bullies, son."

"How's that?"

While Chance had rushed to José's bedside, Dalla
had entered the house and Rosa had told him the res
of the story, the part Chance had failed to stay fo
"According to his wife, the big *norteamericano,* th
leader of this bunch—he was back here not long afte
Manuel left to get you at Twin Rifles," he said. "That'
how José come to look like he come out second best i
a pistol whipping.

"Rosa, she'd rounded up the girl and had her hid
in the fruit cellar. But their boy—Pepe, I think hi
name is—why, he lit right into the fella fighting hi
pa. Feisty young pup, from what I hear."

"That he is," José said with a good deal of pride.

"Anyway, this big fella—he took Pepe with hin
just like that," Dallas said with a quick snap of th
fingers.

"I have heard him called by a name," José saic
"Monroe Marcus, I believe it is."

A clouded look came over Chance's face at th
man's name. As though talking to himself, he mu
tered, "Son of a bitch." Then he bent down slightl
placed a firm hand on José's shoulder, and saic
"Don't you worry, José, we'll get the boy back. An
teach this Monroe Marcus a lesson or two along th
way."

* * *

The evening meal was on the table shortly and Rosa welcomed the company of all four men. She loved to cook and found it easy to make extra food for her guests. But then, as much trail food as Dallas, Chance, Ike, and Manuel had been eating on their way down, it didn't take much to satisfy them. Chance, remember-ng his last trip down here, had packed away a few extra sacks of Arbuckle's coffee. If Rosa could make it stretch, as well he knew she could, they would have coffee for some time to come. They ate in silence and when they were done, Rosa filled their coffee cups one ast time.

"Sure you don't want to leave the old man and come back to Twin Rifles with me, Rosa?" Chance sked in jest. "Miss Margaret could sure use your kind of cooking."

"You know I have a family to tend to." Rosa smiled. he was silent for a moment before her smile widened nd she added, "But if I were twenty years younger or ou twenty years older—ah, then we would have fun."

They all laughed, then she departed, leaving them the talk men take to when the evening meal is done.

"You had a murderous look about you when José entioned that Marcus fella," Dallas commented to Chance. "Name sounds a mite familiar but I don't ecall ever meeting him. Have you?"

"Nope. But I've heard of him all right," Chance aid, the same cross look coming to him now as the rst time he'd heard Monroe Marcus's name.

"Seems to me I heard Wilson and Carny talk about im once in a while," Ike said, now trying to sound ke one of them. "Wasn't he in the war or some-ing?"

"That's a fact." Chance nodded, then stared for a ort while into his coffee cup, as though its depths held the answers he was searching for. "You likely heard his name used right along with that of Quantrill."

"Fella that done in Lawrence, Kansas, back in sixty-three, wasn't it?" Dallas said. "Now that I did hear about. Real scum, ary you ask me."

"Yeah, Marcus is right up there with Quantrill. Started out as a lieutenant to Quantrill, then branched out toward the end of the war and formed his own raider band," Chance said, a grim look about him now. "Tried burning him a couple of towns, too—just like Quantrill—if what I heard was right. I knew he'd come down to Mexico after the war, following Shelby's lead, and was hiring out to the highest bidder." He glanced at José over in the corner and slowly took in the humble surroundings of the adobe building he sat in, chuckling softly to himself. "Man must have fallen on hard times to come together with the comancheros and the Apaches."

"You're expecting trouble from the man then, is that it?" Ike asked, taking a sip of his coffee.

The frustrated look that came over Chance whenever he had been forced to converse with Ike was there once more. "Let's put it this way, Hadley. The man ain't gonna give us nothing but grief. Of that you can be sure."

Ike Hadley suddenly felt as though he had a ball of lead in his stomach, and he didn't like it. Not one bit.

CHAPTER

★ 14 ★

eremiah Younger felt as though he could have been
alking on the very clouds themselves as he carried
arny Wilson's breakfast meal to him that morning.
nd for the life of him, he wasn't sure why it was he
lt that way.

"My, but aren't you chipper, Mr. Younger," Adam
iley said when he let Younger into his office.

The gambler gave the doctor a smile he believed to
e infectious and merely shrugged at the physician's
ords. "Perhaps so, my good man, if that is what you
ll it."

Doc Riley returned the smile. He'd had a decent
ight's sleep in the little room below his office and had
rived at work in a good mood himself. As sketchy a
putation as the Hadley brothers had in this town, he

had learned to trust Wilson Hadley after the second night his brother had taken up space in his extra bedroom. It was evident that Wilson Hadley was concerned with his brother's health more than any drugs or utensils belonging to Adam Riley. So after that second night, which turned out to be a boring one at that—no babies to be delivered, no gunshot wounds or knifings needing his immediate attention—Doc Riley decided to give up playing gin rummy with Wilson Hadley and get some much needed sleep instead. Besides, after the first night Wilson held no real challenge as a card player. But then few people did when they had the welfare of their loved ones constantly on their minds.

It wasn't until Jeremiah saw a disgruntled Wilson Hadley sitting next to his bedridden brother, Carny, that the reason for his happiness hit him. Here were two men, brothers, and one was worrying about the other and probably silently praying for his swift recovery. (One of the many things Jeremiah Younger had learned in coming west was that although prayer was in evident high demand out here, those in need of it tended to utilize it as a last resort. There seemed to be this gigantic belief that a man wasn't a man unless he could take care of himself in this land, God or no God.) He suddenly realized that it reminded him a great deal of the way young Rachel Ferris was feeling about the young man she was so in love with, Chance Carston. And although he thought he'd put it out of his mind for good, it now reminded Jeremiah of how he had stayed by Matty when she was sick, when . . .

"You must eat this right away, good man, for it was piping hot when I left the boardinghouse and—" he started to say, trying to put the thought of his now deceased wife out of his mind.

"You been telling me that every day you bring my
ood to me," Carny said with a growl. It almost
eemed as though the man had a permanent frown on
ais forehead. Either that or he was as sadly in need of
a distemper shot as a mangy cur. Or, on an outside
chance but just as likely, his broken leg was indeed
iving him more pain than he could comfortably
tand. Perhaps so Younger wouldn't think he was
eing singled out, Carny turned his gruff tone on his
rother. "I don't need anyone to watch me eat,
Vilson," he grumbled. "I can still cut and chew fine,
ou know." He tossed off the red checkered cloth
overing the plates of food and added, "So shoo, git
ut of here, the both of you."

If the look on Wilson Hadley's face was any indica-
ion, Jeremiah was sure the older Hadley desperately
vanted to break his younger brother's *other* leg about
ow.

"He does have a temper, doesn't he?" Jeremiah
aid with a rather weak smile. These were two hulk-
ng brothers he was dealing with, these Hadleys.
nd although he stood a couple of inches taller than
ither of them, there was little doubt that each of
iem outweighed him by a good fifty pounds. To
nake things worse, Jeremiah Younger had never
eally considered himself to be a fighter. He hated
ghting, hated war, hated violence of any kind. That
as why he had all but forgotten that hideaway
un, the Derringer, that he had finally pulled on
iose two bullies a couple of days ago. The thought
f having to go up against either one of these Hadley
rothers was a scary one at best for the tall, gangly
ıan. Hence, the weakness in an otherwise pleasant
nile.

"Hell, it ain't that," Wilson said in reply. "That's

Carny's regular disposition. Been that way since he was born and Ma dropped him on his head."

"I daresay it's had a disastrous effect on the man's mouth."

Wilson forced a smile after a moment. "Yeah, it has, ain't it?"

Doc Riley had been called away to one of the local farms, so the two men sat in his outer office in relative silence for several minutes. As he watched a worried Wilson Hadley, it struck Jeremiah Younger that there was something different about his life today. He couldn't put his finger on it, wasn't even sure what had caused it, but there was something different about his disposition. Although he couldn't pinpoint it, he had a sudden urge to help the man sitting in this room with him. Or at least try to. After all, hadn't he just successfully talked Rachel Ferris into believing that her beau would come back safe and sound? And why shouldn't he have said what he did, for he believed the very words that he had spoken. Even after that one meeting, he knew that Chance Carston was one of those young men out here who would claim he was too tough to die. Wilson Hadley probably was, too, but right now he seemed to have an awful lot on his mind.

"Pardon me for acting like a horrid busybody, Mr. Hadley, but may I be so bold as to inquire as to what is bothering you?" he asked, not even sure what he would say next. "Your brother, although I must admit he is a bit mean, does seem to be healthy enough. In fact, were he actually sick, I doubt he would have the energy to act as mean as he does."

Wilson Hadley studied the gambler's face a minute, deep in thought, before opening up to him. "True enough, tinhorn, but it ain't Carny I'm worried about. Hell, I could've left him alone where he fell and he'd

find some way to git by and likely come hobbling into
our place in a week or so, cussing up a storm.

"No, it's that squirt of a brother that's got me worried now." Just bringing up the subject seemed to make him mad and he frowned hard at Jeremiah. "Damn kid got to be a real worrier when Carny took that fall. Got on my nerves on the way back into town, oo, asking over and over, was Carny gonna die, was Carny gonna be all right."

"But why isn't he here if he was that worried about his brother?" Jeremiah asked, a bit confused.

Wilson was silent for a minute, studying his boots before admitting, in a much lower voice than usual, "I run him off."

"What was that, sir? I didn't quite hear you."

"I said I run him off," Wilson said in a growl that was half a roar. Jeremiah heard him loud and clear this time.

"I see." Jeremiah did some quick thinking before adding, "I'm sure he knows it was done in the heat of the moment. I'd not worry about him at all, my friend. If he's as hearty of stock as you Hadleys appear to be, why, you've nothing to worry about."

"How can you be sure?" Wilson asked the man. Other than bringing up his brother's food, the man was a total stranger to him. Still, he seemed concerned and that should count for something, Wilson thought. "How do you know?"

"How old did you say he was?"

"Seventeen."

Jeremiah thought a moment, then chuckled to himself. "You know, I recall when I was about his age. I wanted so much to be recognized by my family, my father and older brothers in particular. Then one day they said I'd be better off without them. Never wanted to cry so badly in my life. But in the middle of the night, I gathered what I could wear or carry and ran away."

"Did you go back?" Wilson found himself mesmerized by the man's story.

"Not for a year. Nor did anyone come after me, which I found to be for the best."

"How's that?"

"Why, don't you see, good man? It wasn't my father and brothers I needed to prove myself to. It was *me* I had to prove I was a man to. Surely you can remember such an experience, can't you?"

Wilson had to dig back in his memory some but finally nodded agreement. "Yeah, I reckon so."

"My guess is your younger brother is likely doing that right now. He would have done it anyway. Your chastising words were just what he needed, the excuse he needed, to go off on his own and find out what kind of man he is." Jeremiah paused to take in some air. "Tell me, is he as big in stature as you and your brother?"

Wilson smiled briefly, remembering how often he'd taken Ike for granted. "No, but he's getting there."

Jeremiah worked that contagious smile of his and said, "Then you have nothing to worry about, my good man. I'm sure he'll be back in fine fettle."

"Tinhorn, you can have your plates back," came the loud voice of Carny from the next room.

"Well, I'd better go," Jeremiah said.

"Thanks for the words, tinhorn," Wilson said. "I appreciate it."

Jeremiah descended the stairs of the doctor's office feeling as though he had indeed been able to help Wilson Hadley some with his problem. He was sure that when he left the man was much better off, far less worried, than when Jeremiah had arrived. He found himself feeling quite good about what he'd accomplished thus far today. Which was why he didn't notice the trouble that awaited him as he rounded the corner of the boardwalk.

"Well, now, what have we got here?" Harry Aker said as Jeremiah Younger all but ran into him. The man had put on a clean pair of pants. With him was his friend, Sam Bayles. "If it ain't the gambler with the hideout gun."

"Why don't you just hand over that peashooter and we'll pick up where we left off last time?" Sam said in his own sarcastic way.

Jeremiah Younger was feeling so good that he was almost tempted to do as the man said, for he honestly believed that nothing or no one could harm him today. Still, he did recall what he had told himself earlier in the morning as these two had left the dining area of the Ferris House. It crossed his mind that perhaps a few questions were in order for these two, the answers to which might very well aid in his finding out just who they were.

He was about to ask a question when Harry Aker ran a big thick hand up Jeremiah's forearm, searching for the derringer rig he knew was located there. It was also about that time that Wilson Hadley rounded the corner and caught up with him in three big strides.

"I hope you ain't doing what it looks like you're doing, friend, 'cause if you are, you're in a heap of trouble." Wilson Hadley sounded as raspy-voiced and gruff as his brother had, and there was no bluff in his words.

Harry Aker tried sounding like there wasn't any bluff in his tone of voice, too, but it didn't come off so well. "And who the hell are you?"

"Why, the tinhorn here—I mean Younger—he's my best friend," Wilson said. "I heard what you two pulled the other day. Don't mind telling you I ain't too fond of it, either. You try to give old Jeremiah here a hard time and I'm likely to—"

"Now just what in the devil is a-going on?" Joshua Holly, the town deputy marshal, said as he came upon the group. "Must be something, 'cause you're sounding almighty loud to me."

"Oh, it was nothing, Deputy," Jeremiah said, trying to pass the incident off. "Just a minor misunderstanding, I assure you."

But Wilson Hadley wasn't about to let it go. It wasn't often he was on the right side of anything, so when he was he made the most of it. "Fact of the matter is, Deputy, these two was about to see how far they could push old Jeremiah here."

"Well, now, is that a fact?"

"That it is." Wilson Hadley's voice hadn't gotten any softer since the arrival of Joshua. If anything, it got harder and louder. "I just come along and seen what was happening and started reading to 'em from the book."

"You did, eh?" Joshua, like most everyone else in Twin Rifles, knew that the Hadleys had less knowledge of what was in the Good Book than anyone else in the territory. It was just the way they were. Everyone knew that. "And just what was it you was figgering on doing next, ary I might ask?"

"Well, Joshua, the truth of the matter is, it's a good thing you come along. Yes it is," Wilson said with raised eyebrow.

"Oh. And how's that?"

Wilson glanced at Aker and Bayles first, tossed a short glance at Joshua, then down at his six-gun in its ıolster. He undid the thong on the hammer as he said, 'I was just about to show 'em the pictures."

Joshua Holly's eyes nearly bulged as he got the idea f what Wilson Hadley was talking about. "Oh, no ou don't!" he said in a voice close to flustered. "They in't a-gonna be no shooting matches in this town! Vhy, that much blood would make a body sick as ould be. No, sir. You take them guns outta here ary ou want to shoot 'em."

"And if we don't?" Harry Aker said, a sneer coming his face.

"Why, I'll shoot you, of course!" Joshua said, and ulled out his own six-gun, training it on the two oublemakers. "Now, you just git afore I git nervous r something."

If Jeremiah Younger was having a fine day, Harry ker and Sam Bayles were experiencing a day that asn't worth spit.

CHAPTER
★ 15 ★

Dallas Bodeen found himself feeling a good deal like mother hen. Of the three men he could call ridin pards, only Ike Hadley was having little if any trouble After Rosa had fixed them the evening meal, Ike an Rosa's daughter had a good time playing in th backyard. Most of what they played were children' games to be sure—tag and hide-and-seek and the like But it was fun they were having, both acting a carefree as if they were five years old again. In fact Dallas had noticed that as the evening wore or seventeen-year-old Ike was taking quite a fancy t young Maria. But then, Maria—who was all of four teen, according to her mother—had reached that ag when the simple cotton shirts she wore had begun t grow a bit tight. And a young man like Ike, well, h was sure to notice that sort of growth in a relatively shy young lady like Maria.

Still, it wasn't Ike who had bothered Dallas that night. It was Chance. And it all started when Chance asked José and Rosa more about the yahoos who were giving them the trouble.

"I don't mean those comancheros or the tight-lipped Apache," he'd said in a curious tone. "I'm talking about this fella you keep referring to as the *norteamericano.* You'd think there was a million of 'em, as many as you see heading south of the border these days. Besides, this fella's got my interest."

"Ah, *el norteamericano,"* José said with a nod of the head. "Monroe Marcus." José became suddenly serious as the subject of his attacker came up. "He is a mean one, that hombre." His focus shifted to Manuel as he continued. "It was two days after you left, Manuel, that he returned with his *compadres.* If Rosa hadn't seen them first, we might all be dead now. It was she who was able to hide Maria in the root cellar. And you have seen Maria. She is . . . well, she is . . ."

"Real healthy," Chance said, knowing the man must feel embarrassed trying to describe his only daughter.

"She is a flower in bloom," Rosa said with the ease only a mother can have in expressing the coming of womanhood.

"I was about to say that," Dallas said.

"Well, señor, *the norteamericano*—this Marcus—he would think much more and do much worse had he found her." José's tone turned to one of anger now as he recalled the incident. He need say no more for those with him to understand that he was speaking of what might have been the rape of his daughter.

"What made 'em come back so soon?" Dallas

asked, a frown forming over one eye. "I thought yo
told me earlier that this crew didn't bother you bu
once in a while?"

"Es verdad, señor." Once again his concentratio
shifted to his brother-in-law, the hard look with it
"They returned because they had stopped Manuel an
warned him against going any further on his journey
It was then they beat me and took my son."

All eyes turned to Manuel when José was finishe
speaking, and although they were not accusatory i
any respect, they might as well have been. At least t
Manuel. The Mexican knew he had failed, knew it wa
his fault that José had suffered a second beating, hi
fault that his nephew Pepe had been taken hostage
Seated at the table, he made a quick effort to stan
and found himself grunting at the pain he still carrie
in his side. But that pain was nothing compared t
what he felt in his heart, and he forced himself to ris
to two feet and make his way out of the adob
structure as quickly as possible. It was time for a ma
to be alone, to think of his mistakes.

"Manuel!" José yelled in as adequate a voice as h
could muster. Dallas rose from his chair, ready to g
after the man.

"No," Rosa said in a firm tone as she held a hand u
to him to stop. "I will tend to him. It must be his sid
that aches," she added, although they all knew it wa
much more serious than that. But then that is th
length of kindness that comes from women.

"Sometimes I fear that I say the wrong thing," Jos
said by way of apology.

"Don't feel bad, hoss, I do it a hell of a lot my ow
self," Chance said with half a smile.

"Ain't that the goddamn truth," Dallas muttered i
more of a statement than a question.

"Don't you worry, José. First light tomorrow we'll be on their trail. We'll have your boy back for you in no time flat," Chance said with confidence.

José, who still lay in his bed, placed a warm hand on Chance's arm, only partially gripping it before the big man could leave. In a smile filled with pain, he said, "*El ranger tejano,* eh? I am glad you have come, *mi amigo.* So glad."

Chance knew the importance of what José was saying, especially to the man himself. He returned the smile and said, "I'd do it for any man I call a friend, and I've got a notion you already know that."

José smiled again, perhaps a bit less in pain now hat he had the big man's reassurance.

It was outside, soon after the day had turned to larkness, that Dallas found Chance with a somewhat vorried look about him.

"You look about as worried as José," he said. He vasn't even sure Chance would want to talk to him bout what was on his mind, especially considering ne way he'd treated him after that Indian fight. Truth o tell, Dallas wouldn't blame Chance if he never poke to him again. After all, he couldn't recall ever neeting up with anyone who had as much pride as hance Carston—unless, of course, it was himself. Care to chew the fat over it a mite?"

Either Chance had decided to confide in the old nountain man, even though he irked him, or Dallas odeen's words out on the trail had sunk in and he ad forgiven the older man. Either way, there was oubt in his face when he turned to Dallas.

"You ever have a notion when you set out on a nission that you might not be coming back?" Chance ked in a serious tone. "Ever have that happen to ou?"

"Oh, sure, a couple of times," Dallas replied. H
didn't have to reach too far back in his memory to pul
out an example, either. "Why, I recall the spring o
thirty-two, when we went down to rendezvous. Ha
the damnedest notion that I'd not be seeing some o
my friends again. Fact is, for a while there I had i
figured I'd be the one cashing in my plew."

Chance was quiet for a while before asking, "Any
thing ever come of it?"

Dallas almost bugged his eyes out in disbelief. "I'l
say! Why, that Pierre's Hole fiasco was one of th
worst I was ever in, by God! And I did lose me
handful of friends, too. Them Big Bellies—them Gro
Ventres—why, they had us in their sights that day
Important thing was I didn't cash in no plew, for I'n
the one who's a-telling the story. But, as I said, I di
lose a few good friends."

Again Chance was silent, looking out into th
coming darkness, as though to find an answer to hi
problems. "Well, believe it or not, Dallas, I've had th
same feeling about this little adventure, ever since w
left Twin Rifles. Hell, these characters we're going u
against sound like quite a bunch, if you listen to Jos
and Rosa."

Dallas shrugged. "You've been up against wors
before, ary my recollect is right."

"Yeah, but look what I'm dealing with this time.
seventeen-year-old kid that ain't got no idea of wha
manhood is, much less able to shoot a six-gun,
Mexican with a busted side, and—" Here he pause
for he knew that the only one left to describe wa
Dallas Bodeen, and after having been knocked flat o
his keister by the man, he wasn't too eager to see if i
could be done again.

"And a worn-out old mountain man," Dallas sai

ooking him straight in the eye as he spoke. "Yeah, I know what I am, son. But then, I reckon that's what comes with age. You git to face reality with a bit nore . . . reality."

"Look, Dallas, I didn't mean to—"

"You know what your problem is, Chance? You're ust getting old enough to get a taste of that reality, the ind that tells you that you're human after all. The ind that tells you that sometimes when you get shot, why, you don't get up right away.

"Trouble with you youngsters is that when that egins to happen to you, why, you start seeing ghosts hat weren't there before. And I'll tell you something, onny, ary you pay too much attention to 'em, you'll vind up being one of 'em pretty quick."

Dallas paused for a moment, as though to take in a eep breath. "And I know a young brunette back in Twin Rifles who'd get madder than hell at you if you vas to let yourself die before she could marry you."

"You mean, you know about—" Chance started to ay in astonishment.

"Shoot, boy, the whole town knows you two are uck on one another like taffy on an apple," Dallas aid with a sly grin. "Truth is we got us a pool going ver to Ernie Johnson's Saloon as to who asks who rst, you or her."

Dallas never was sure if it was his speechifying or s humor that changed Chance's disposition that ght, but it did.

"Smart ass," Chance said with a grin when he went side.

"Hell, at least I admit it," Dallas tossed after him, ways getting in the last word. That too seemed to be ne of the privileges of age.

* * *

The night had passed and Dallas was the first one t meet Rosa in her kitchen area the following morning She already had a pot of the black stuff brewing, so th old mountain man went out in the early morning gra light and, waking up to the cool night air that stil lingered about, brought in another armful of wood fo Rosa.

They were still alone when she poured him a cup o coffee and he asked, "How's Manuel doing?"

"I'm afraid his pride is hurt much more than an bones he may have broken," she said to him, knowin what he was getting at.

"I reckon pride's pretty important to a man ou here," he said, downing some more of the hot stuf "Lot of times it's all he's got to keep him going, righ or wrong."

"*Sí*, but it has affected my brother so that he no acts the part of a fool," she said with force.

"A fool? Now what in the devil brought that on?"

"Because of what my husband said last nigh Manuel now believes that Pepe being taken a hostag is his fault."

"But how's that—"

"You will see, my friend, you will see."

Sure enough, everyone was soon up and eating the table, including Manuel. No one said anythin until after the meal, when they were ready to leave.

Outside, Ike Hadley brought out the horses fc Chance, Dallas, and himself. He also had the extı horse with him, the idea being that they would need for Pepe once they freed him from Monroe Marcu and his crowd. They didn't see Manuel head for th barn and return shortly, the reins of his own horse i his hand.

"And where the hell do you think you're going?" Chance asked with a frown. It was obvious that he lidn't want any wounded men along with him on this excursion into hell.

"Why, I am going with you, of course," the Mexican aid with a smile. "After all, it is my nephew you are going to rescue, is it not?"

José had made his way to the front door, using a ong stick as a cane to support his side as he leaned gainst the door. "Manuel, you must stay here," he aid. "You are almost as badly hurt as I. You will only e a burden to these men," he added, and immediately regretted his words.

If it was possible to be sad and angry at the same me, Manuel had achieved that combination. They ould all see that it took a great deal of strength to imply mount his saddle, but none was going to stop ie man from having his say. "I seem to be a burden to veryone of late," he said, mustering energy from ithin. "But perhaps that is only part of the problem, osé. Perhaps the other part of the problem is that I ave done nothing but what you say. I wonder if that n't why I lack the courage of your friends." He riefly glanced at Chance, Ike, and Dallas. "No more. his time I will do what I want to do. Perhaps then I ill succeed at something."

"No one questions your courage, Manuel," José id.

"You did," the Mexican replied in a cold, hard tone. could see it in your eyes last night."

"Who will help with the defense here?" José asked. cannot stand here at the door all day."

"Got a rifle?" Chance asked, turning his gaze to osa.

"Yes, but I'm not much good with it," she replied meekly.

Chance frowned a moment in thought, then dismounted and went to the extra horse Ike held the reins to. Bundled at the rear of the saddle were the same rifles they had used in the Indian fight only a day or two back. For one brief glance, he took in the butt stocks all sticking out, then made his choice and grabbed one in the middle. By the time he had pulled it out, he nodded and walked to Rosa, murmuring, "Tighten that bundle" to Ike before he left.

Presenting a sawed-off shotgun to Rosa, Chance smiled and said, "They developed this gun for people who are too skittish to hunt with a single-shot rifle. Long as your game is close in, it's hard to miss when you fire this at 'em. Just cock the hammers, plant the butt stock on your hip, point the barrel at 'em, and pull the trigger."

"And if I miss?" Rosa still wasn't certain she could fire the weapon effectively.

"If you miss, sister, I wouldn't worry too awful much," Dallas said with a straight face. "The concussion will likely kill him."

"I see," she said, looking at the shotgun with a good deal of awe and respect.

Back in the saddle, Chance looked at Manuel. "You sure you want to do this, amigo?"

"I have to, señor," Manuel said. "Just like you, I have my pride." He glanced quickly at José and added, "Finally."

"Suits me," Chance said.

"Vaya con Dios, amigos," José and Rosa said almost at the same time.

Ike Hadley, who had been surprisingly quiet this morning, said, "You do the praying, ma'am, and we'll do the shooting. We can likely use a mite of help from the Man Upstairs."

"Amen, brother," Dallas said.

Then they rode off.

CHAPTER

★ 16 ★

To Jeremiah Younger's surprise, Wilson Hadley be
gan to take his meals with him on a regular basis
Morning, noon, or night, Wilson would show u
within five minutes of the time the tall gamble
entered the Ferris House and took a seat for a meal
Perhaps it was because Jeremiah had turned out to b
a rather predictable person. He would show u
promptly at six for the morning and evening repas
and at noon sharp for his midday meal. Like many
local citizen who had gotten a taste of the offerings c
the Ferris women, he made sure to take a first seat a
any given meal. After all, with cooking this popula
the food was likely to be gone in no time.

On the other hand was the fact that Wilson couldn
recall eating too regular out at the place they calle

home. There had been times when he hadn't eaten at
all simply because there wasn't enough food to go
around for the five brothers. And being the oldest, it
was he who had passed on the meager amounts of
food they might have. So when Carny was brought on
with this difficulty of his, Wilson had made the
decision he would catch up on his meal eating. When
he'd decided to keep track of Jeremiah Younger and
his goings on, he had dug out a twenty-dollar gold
piece—over half of the money he could lay claim to at
the moment—plunked it in Rachel's hand, and said,
"I'll eat on this till it runs out, ma'am—then you just
tell me I ain't welcome anymore." The words had so
startled Rachel that Wilson Hadley was gone before
she could think of anything to say.

"I see that you, too, enjoy the fare in this establishment," Jeremiah said when he found the older Hadley
seated next to him for the second day in a row.

Wilson gave the gambler a sideward glance before
saying, "Grub's tasty all right. But actually, I figured
to keep an eye on you while you're delivering my
brother's meals to him. Carny always has had a hunger
about him, and I ain't too fond of them two pecker-
woods that taken to hoorawing you."

Jeremiah put down his fork, a blush working itself
up his neck. "I must say again that you showed up at a
most opportune time the other day. If you hadn't,
why, I would have been in dire straits indeed," he
said, his face in full flush by the time the words were
out.

"Oh, hell, it weren't nothing. Why, I can remember
days when me and Carny was mostly like that, too,"
Wilson said, dismissing the incident. Then he totally
ignored anything else Jeremiah might have wanted to
say and went back to eating his meal. He hadn't been

lying by any stretch of the imagination when he'd said the food here was good, but it was a whole lot better when it was hot.

As usual, Jeremiah left the Ferris House carrying a tray of food for Carny that morning. Whether it was planned that way or not, he didn't know, but he and Wilson met Harry Aker and Sam Bayles walking toward them on the boardwalk. At first Jeremiah was expecting more trouble, but the closer they got, the more the two seemed to be ignoring him—or was it Wilson?—as they looked away.

"Good morning, gentlemen," Jeremiah said in a cheerful manner.

Neither man responded, which was when Wilson, who had been walking behind Jeremiah, stuck out a big hand and stopped the lead man in his tracks. "He's talking to you, pilgrim," he said in a raspy tone. That was one thing Wilson Hadley had going for him. From the tone of his voice, which was always raspy and gruff, it was hard telling when he was talking regular and when he was feeling piss-ugly mean.

"Take your hand off me," Harry Aker said in a forceful manner of his own, apparently not at all intimidated by the big man before him now. But Wilson Hadley decided it was time this man had the fear of God put into him.

At first he had only placed the palm of his huge hand flat-out on Harry Aker's chest, easily stopping him in midstep. Now he grabbed a fistful of the man's shirt and tossed him against the wall of the storefront they were passing. When he did, the false front shook. Wilson Hadley wasn't fast with a gun, not like Chance Carston and some others he'd seen and heard about, but he managed to get by. At the same time he was rattling Harry Aker's tree, he used his free hand t pull out his Remington .44 and stick it out within about six inches of Sam Bayles's stomach.

"I hope you ain't thinking of getting out of line, mister, 'cause I really ain't in the mood for it today," he said, throwing the man a frown that was as mean as his words.

Sam Bayles paused for a moment, obviously out of ear of not seeing the sun set that day. "Like you say, t's too early for this stuff today." With a nod toward eremiah, he said, "Morning, gambler," and was on is way without another word.

Harry Aker took a hint from his riding pard and ollowed in silence.

"Please, Mr. Hadley, if you continue to display this ort of zeal, I'm afraid the rafters will tumble down on s," Jeremiah said, glancing up at the shaky rafters ver the boardwalk. With a smile he added, "Then hat will your brother think of the meal service in this own?"

Wilson Hadley seemed to have lost his sense of umor and said nothing the rest of the way to Doc iley's office. He sat in relative silence as Jeremiah erved Carny his morning meal and left the room so e man could eat alone, which he seemed to prefer.

"If you don't mind my asking, Wilson, what is it at made you change?" Jeremiah asked when he ntered the physician's outer office.

"Huh?"

"Why wasn't it you down there taking advantage of e instead of those plug uglies? What made you ange your ways?"

Seated, Wilson Hadley did little more than stare at e hat in his hand, and he did it for what seemed to the longest time. "Ain't sure, really. Maybe it was st getting tired of being lonely for so long.

"Me and Carny, we'd find enough money for bottle and drink it quick as you please," Wilso continued. "Then we'd head on into town. I reckon w were meaning to be social with the crowd but it neve did turn out that way. Always got us a fight going an wound up getting thrown out of town by the marsha Got so bad he'd pull his gun soon as he saw us rid into town, even if we were dead sober.

"No, sir, drinking and fighting was about all w could do. And I don't mind telling you that it gc goddamn lonely after a while."

"And you decided to become part of the solutio instead of the problem?" Jeremiah said, trying t second-guess what the man was getting at.

"I reckon you could call it that." The tone in Wilso Hadley's voice had softened considerably, eve though it was still raspy to the ear. It was as though h were saying something to this man that he had neve said to another human being in his lifetime. And fc the life of him, Wilson was hard put to calculate why was he was spilling his guts to this tinhorn gamble All he knew for sure was that the man seemed to ca about him and that was a feeling he hadn't exper enced in some time.

He went on to tell Jeremiah about the time a year c two back when he and Carny had sought out Parde Taylor, who had been known for many a year as th town drunk and bully. He knew that anyone he aske in town about trying to learn manners, why, the would laugh him right out of Twin Rifles. So h hunted up Pardee, a man younger than he but a ma who had somehow straightened himself out and wa gathering at least a bit of respect in town. It had take the better part of a week, but Pardee had shown the he right way to act in town, the right way to speak to ›eople, especially the womenfolk. It was Thanksgiv-ng Day, the end of that week he'd spent with the ›ldest Hadley brothers, that Pardee had taken them nto Twin Rifles and they had attended church ser-'ices.

A hint of a smile came to Wilson's lips and he said, 'Had near everyone in the church staring at us, not elieving the Almighty would ever admit a Hadley to hurch."

Jeremiah smiled, too, trying to bring some humor › the situation. "I suppose the marshal had his eye on ou, too?"

Wilson chuckled to himself. "Actually, old Will 'arston had his hand on his gun through the whole ɛrvice. Didn't trust us worth a whit. But we showed ɛm, we did. Busted up a fight that day. And would ou believe it, why, it was one we *didn't* start!"

Jeremiah gave his best smile of confidence. "Good ›r you, Wilson Hadley." He seemed sure that his 'ords would give this rough-hewn man some encour-ʒement, but Hadley still looked rather glum. "You now, Wilson, often when we make decisions in life, e find them hard to live with. I've found in my fetime that the only thing that ever really makes ıem easier to live with is the certain faith we have in ırselves that we have done the right thing. If it's ›nfirmation you lack . . . well, I for one think you've ›ne the right thing."

"All right, tinhorn, here's your plates," came arny's loud voice from the next room.

Jeremiah picked up the tray and empty plates and as about to make his way toward the exit to Doc iley's office when he heard Wilson say, "You know,

Jeremiah, one of the reasons I don't mind bein around you is that I like to hear you talk. Mostly, yo make a lot of sense."

The tall man smiled. "Well, I'm flattered, Wilson and I thank you for those kind words. Believe me, discovered long ago that the kind words in this worl are few and far between."

"Yeah, I reckon you're right."

Jeremiah dismissed himself and headed for th door. He had just opened the door when he stopped i his tracks and turned to face Wilson. The look abou him was that of a man who has philosophized abou something and come to a conclusion about it.

"You know, Wilson, I once knew a man who mad the claim that any man who went a decade withou changing his mind at least once on something . . well, he ought to be declared brain dead," Jeremia said, only half smiling.

"Is that a fact?" Wilson Hadley replied with th same half smile.

"Oh, yes, indeed. I say that, of course, becaus considering the amount of things you've changed you mind about, well, my good man, you must be quit intelligent."

Wilson Hadley couldn't believe the words he'd jus heard as he watched Jeremiah Younger leave.

CHAPTER

★ 17 ★

They trailed Marcus Monroe and his companions to
ıe west. A wind had blown away some of the tracks
nce they were made, but Dallas, who did most of the
acking because he was best at it, had been able to
ursue the hoof print left by one of the heavier riders.
rom what José had said, he gauged that to be the
omanchero, for the *norteamericano* had been de-
icted as a tall, lean fellow. The comanchero's horse
ad a definitive mark on its right front shoe, a
ademark indentation that might have been made on
e outer portion of the shoe by a blacksmith's hasp.
ll he knew was that it was noticeable and easy to
llow, and that was good enough for Dallas Bodeen.
The trail ran straight west for most of that day and
ey made good time following it. Water holes were

scarce until sunset and they used up both canteens o water each man carried. If it hadn't been for th shortage of water and the water hole they came acros at day's end, Dallas was sure Chance would hav pushed on toward the kidnappers until way pas sundown.

Making sure everyone had a good ration of wate the second day, they set out following the same set o tracks. By midmorning the heat was a concern t them, but Chance insisted that they push on. The didn't break for a dry noon camp, once again pushin on at Chance's insistence. It was midafternoon whe Dallas came upon a small water hole and reined in hi mount.

"That's it, Chance," he said as he dismounted fror his saddle. "Me and this hoss ain't a-going no farthe atall. I've heard it said that ary the saddle creaks, i ain't paid for, but I'm here to tell you that creaky a they are, both my saddle and my bones been paid fo many a time over."

"Know what you mean, Dallas," Ike said, als dismounting. "Think I lost the feeling in my ass abou ten miles back." With little concern as to what Chanc might have to say, he loosened the cinch on his mour and led it to the water hole, as sparse as its offering might be.

Manuel took his time getting out of the saddle an followed suit.

Chance didn't say anything. But then, the look o his face said just about everything he was feeling. Lik Dallas, he had been a Texas Ranger and, like Dalla he was used to being listened to, used to being i charge of the situation. But at the moment he wasn sure whether the old mountain man was testing him t see if old age outranked middle age, or if the old cuss simply couldn't go any further and had decided to dismount and take a breather. He personally doubted here was any reason that Dallas Bodeen would ever stop riding or tracking in that manner. The look on he face of Chance was filled with only one thing—pure frustration.

It was when the horses had taken their drinks and he four had refilled their canteens that they got the care of their lives. They were tightening their cinches when they looked up and saw a band of Indians that had quietly surrounded them and were ready to use heir weapons if need be.

"Kickapoo, I'd say," Dallas commented to his companions as he raised his hand in peace to the pparent leader of the group and proceeded to talk to he tribe in sign language. "Seems they're as curious bout what we're doing as we are about them," he dded in a few minutes.

"Tell 'em we're after a kidnapping son of a bitch," Chance said with a snarl. "Monroe Marcus is his ame, if it makes any difference. Tell 'em that."

Dallas relayed Chance's words. The leader of the ndian group raised a crooked eyebrow and went rough the motions of sign language. Dallas quickly iscovered that these Kickapoo seemed to hate the x-Confederate soldier just as much as the former angers did. "From what I gather, ary they had anted posters on Marcus they'd be nailing 'em to any ee you could find in this desert land," he said to hance, Ike, and Manuel. "As it is, I reckon they'll st kill the son of a bitch on sight."

"Looks like we all got something in common," Ike id, smiling at a brave seated atop his pony across from him. You'd have thought he was wanting t make friends with the lad, who didn't appear an older than Ike himself.

The leader of the bunch of warriors turned his pon away, looked back over his shoulder, and waved on arm for Chance and his friends to follow him.

Chance shook his head and gave Dallas a glance "Tell him I ain't got no time for a powwow or pip smoking or anything else. I got a notion we ain't al that far from Monroe Marcus and his friends. Besides the sooner we get to 'em, the sooner we'll be able to ge Pepe back."

"I'll tell him, Chance, but I got a notion, too," Dallas said.

"Oh?"

"Yeah. I got me a notion he ain't gonna take to kindly to having his invite turned down, no matte how much of a hurry you're in." When Chance gav him a hard look, the old mountain man added "Believe me, son, I been dealing with the Indians on this frontier longer than you've been walking thi earth and I know what I'm talking about." Fo emphasis, Dallas gave a glance to Ike and Manuel "Why, ary you can believe it, these buggers can be helluva lot more temperamental than Chance if the want."

Ike and Manuel smiled at Dallas's words. With shrug, the Mexican said, "I have no quarrel with thes men."

"Me neither," Ike added. "Hell, if we're as close t that kidnapper as Chance says, we oughtta be able t catch up with him right quick once we finish wit these fellas."

So the four of them followed the Kickapoo on wha turned out to be a southerly course for all of two mile efore coming on their camp. As Indian camps went, his one wasn't all that large, with maybe twenty or hirty tepees to it if what Chance gauged was correct.

"I was you, I'd hang them *pistolas* of yours on your addle horn," Dallas said when they were in camp and lismounting. He shoved the Henry rifle he'd been arrying inside the bedroll behind his saddle. "You let em know you trust 'em, and it's a sure bet your ix-shooters will be here when you get ready to ride ut."

For once Chance did as Dallas suggested without an rgument.

Inside a tepee all four of them were introduced to ne tribal leader, Chief Papequah, and Dallas once gain found himself using sign language to explain ho they were and what their mission was—why they ere down in this country. When the chief heard what eir mission was, he no longer had any qualms about tting them roam the land. Dallas said as much to hance, adding, "After all, any man who has Monroe larcus for an enemy cannot be all bad. That's a direct uote from the chief."

Chance digested the information but didn't seem tisfied with all he had heard. "Something don't em right here," he said to the old mountain man, a ight frown covering his face. "If it's just Marcus, the manchero, and the Apache, why don't the Kickapoo ipe 'em out? Hell, they must have thirty or forty arriors in camp by my guess."

Dallas relayed Chance's concerns to Chief apequah and wound up raising a curious eyebrow nen he heard the Kickapoo leader's reply.

"Something wrong?" Chance asked, seeing the un-rtainty in his partner's face.

"I'll say," Dallas said with a sigh. "According to the

chief, it ain't just these three yahoos we been trackin
that makes up Marcus's outfit. It appears he's go
himself upwards of a dozen men who are good wit
guns. That does tend to stack the odds against us
don't you think?"

"So it would seem," Chance said, a worried loo
coming across his own face now. He was silent for
moment, as though in thought, before saying, "Wha
about Ike and Manuel?"

Dallas knew exactly what Chance was talkin
about. "Wouldn't blame 'em a bit if they went bac
home and looked on this as a bad experience."

"How about you?"

Dallas frowned, taking on a dead-serious look as h
glared at Chance Carston. "Now, son, you kno
better than to even come that close to calling me
quitter. I come along for the whole ride—buckin
shooting, and all."

Even in the darkness of Chief Papequah's tepe
Dallas thought he could see Chance's face turn
bright shade of red. "Should have known better,
reckon," Chance said.

"Don't you worry none about me and Manuel," Ik
said in a firm voice. "We'll be here till the end, an
that, friend, is that."

"Sí," Manuel said with a nod of agreement.

Again there was a silence among them befor
Chance spoke. "That still don't seem right, you kno
Even with a dozen men, the chief and his tribe mu
outnumber 'em three or four to one. Why don't the
just wipe the lot of 'em out?"

Dallas translated Chance's words and did a lot o
nodding and listening as Chief Papequah related wh
turned out to be a rather sorrowful story.

Dallas Bodeen did indeed know a good deal abo

he Indians that ranged from the Canadian Rockies to Sonora, but what the chief told him was a combina-ion of tribal history that one is proud of in places and speaks little of in others.

The word *kickapoo* meant "he moves about, stand-ng now here, now there" in the Algonquin language. t seemed to fit for a tribe that had turned out to be as omadic as they were. Originally, they had resided in vhat was now Wisconsin, moving south into the resent states of Illinois and Indiana somewhere round 1765. The tribe had fought against the United tates in the Second Revolutionary War—or what ome were calling the War of 1812—and assisted the ederal government fighting against the Seminoles in he Black Hawk War. As the white man continued to ove in and take over their lands, factions of the ibes would move on to other places. In 1852 a large and of Kickapoo had migrated down into Mexico, hile others of the tribe moved to Missouri and ortheastern Kansas.

"This is where it gits kinda sketchy, hoss," Dallas id with caution, wanting to make sure he got the ibe's history right. "The chief and what he had of his ibe was moving out of the Indian Territory and ading down to Mexico early in sixty-five. Figured it as 'bout time to join that bigger band that moved own here in fifty-two, I reckon. He ain't too particu-r about the whys and wherefores of the move, and I dn't ask.

"Comes on Dove Creek off the South Concho River d, quick as you can snap your finger, why, he's being rred on by Texas State volunteers. Mistook 'em for omanches, is what they done. Turns out he lost him me men, but he taught them border volunteers a ing or two about attacking the Kickapoo. Had a

couple hundred in his band then, and they was wel
armed too."

"Where are they now?" Chance asked.

"More 'n half of 'em's took off for that larger banc
that settled down here," Dallas said. "The chief—he'
got mebbe thirty warriors and a good share of th
women and kids."

"I still don't understand what he's looking so sa
for," Chance asked in a curious way.

"I noticed the same thing, hoss. Asked him 'bout it
too. After dealing with the Comanches most of you
life, I reckon this will sound as strange as can be. Bu
the man says he's wanting to live in peace," Dalla
said, motioning his head toward Chief Papequah
"Trouble is, after that shoot-out at Dove Creek, why
every time he sees a white man he's afraid they'll ligh
into him. You know, mistake him for a Comanch
again. Don't figure he'll ever find him peace. And h
ain't too keen on the rifles and pistols the white ma
uses for killing, either. He was real definite on that
Chance."

"What's he find so hateful about Monroe Marcus?
Chance asked.

"Now, that one's a mite easier to digest. Seems he'
having the same troubles with this Marcus fella tha
Manuel and his family is," Dallas said. "Bully that h
is, the man just rides into camp, displaying all sorts o
rifles and pistols and such, and demands what eatin
food they got left. It's that or git killed, I reckon.
Before Chance could ask any more questions, Dalla
added, "Chief's only got him a couple of repeate
rifles and they's out of ammunition. Other than tha
it's bows and arrows, and hunting knives, and toma
hawks they got to defend theyselves. I get the notio

hese fire-spitting weapons of Marcus and his men is eal scary things. If you get my drift."

Chance nodded. "I think I understand."

"If this is their camping grounds, maybe they got an dea where this Marcus fella can be found," Ike said, s though thinking out loud. "Could save us from iding these horses to death or riding into a trap, if he vants to see his way clear to give us a hand putting this o-good bastard out of business."

Chance was taken aback with surprise at the young nan's words. "Damn, son, there may be hope for you et. That's not a bad idea at all."

"What's on your mind?" Dallas asked Chance.

"Ask the chief what he thinks about loaning out a rave, if he really does know where Marcus might be amping out," was Chance's reply. "If he's got some raves who know how to use a repeater, tell him we've ot us a couple of extra guns that'll even the odds gainst Marcus if he wants to throw in with us."

By the time Dallas was through translating, it was l too evident that Chief Papequah would do what he ould to help rid the earth of the likes of Monroe .arcus.

CHAPTER
★ 18 ★

José Quesada had picked the right words when he' described Monroe Marcus as tall and lean, for th ex-Confederate-turned-outlaw was just that. Althoug not quite as thick in the chest as Chance Carston, h could definitely match the man in height, standin well over six feet tall.

Like more than one man who had come away fro the war and been unable to hold down a steady jo Monroe Marcus had taken to being a profession bully as a way of life. And why not bully the world, a long as it would give you what you demanded? For th last four years he had gotten everything he wanted b simply threatening to kill whomever it was he wa taking it from. After all, a man had to be good a omething, and Monroe Marcus was definitely good at his. And why shouldn't he be?

He hadn't been the schoolteacher that William C. Quantrill had been before the war taught him a lifferent profession, but Marcus had served with Quantrill the first two and a half years he was with the Confederacy and had learned plenty. In fact, he had een with Quantrill at Lawrence, Kansas, in the fall of 53, when they had burned the town to the ground and illed over a hundred of its residents. *Be bold and take hat you want* was what he had learned from Quan-ill and his raiders. It wasn't long after the affair in Kansas that Monroe Marcus had struck out on his wn and formed his own raider group. He couldn't onvince the James and Younger brothers to ride with im when he left, but along the way he'd found some ıen who might otherwise be considered misfits if it eren't for the fact that they could shoot the hair off a ea at a hundred yards. And none of them had ever ıd the courage to challenge him, so the complete ontrol he had over this group gave him that much ore confidence in his own abilities.

The war had never really ended for many of the onfederate soldiers. Word had gotten around that Jo ıelby had taken his command south of the border. ıd when Colonel Monroe Marcus, as he'd chris-ned himself upon activating his own raider group ıring the war, discovered that some folks would put with his shenanigans only so long, why, he and his en had picked up and headed south of the border as ell. Infused with the belief that there was big money be made in fighting for Maximilian—or Benito árez and the ragtag army he opposed—Marcus and men were sure they had found their pot of gold.

But the war was going badly when they had arrive
and any gold Maximilian might have had was by no
spirited away to wherever he might flee into exil
That left them with little more than the damned peon
of the country, and they had nothing at all.

Marcus had fallen back on doing what he knew h
was good at and tried to fend off some of the warlord
who ran the surrounding territory, the idea being th
perhaps he could impress them and they would joi
him in his planned plundering. But the warlor
wanted nothing at all to do with Marcus and he ha
gone from sixteen men in his fold to just over a doze
now. He'd forgotten that he was dealing with thes
men in their own territory and that could be
dangerous thing to do. That mistake had cost hi
three of his men, and he now had only thirteen me
plus himself.

Thus the great Monroe Marcus had been brought t
rousting the local farmers for whatever grub an
supplies he needed, threatening men like Jos
Quesada, who seldom did more than back down. H
had discovered during the war that men with famili
seldom wanted to fight, seldom wanted to take
chance on getting themselves and their families kille
So most of the time they would hand over what h
told them he wanted. Usually it was enough to feed h
men for a week or so. Of late he had even starte
preying on some of the local Indian tribes once h
learned they wanted only peace.

It was when he'd raided the Quesada farm and the
discovered the hired hand riding away in such
desperate manner that he decided he would teac
them a lesson. Peons like this had to be shown the
place, especially when they supplied you with some
the better eating in the territory. He had warned th

lready scared Mexican about going any further to get ielp, for Marcus knew that was where he was headed. After all, he was scared, right? But when they'd beaten im and he had gone on anyway, well, Monroe Marcus had decided that these people needed to be aught a lesson. It was then he'd ridden back to the Quesada place and proceeded to beat the old man and ake the boy with him. He had yet to decide just what e would do with the boy, trouble that he was. Kill im? Perhaps. Or maybe simply beat the hell out of im, maybe cripple him a bit, and return him to his amily as a warning of things to come if they dared hallenge his authority again. It was when he saw aco, a half-breed who served as his right-hand man, iat he began to lean heavily toward killing the boy utright.

"Damn that little bastard," the half-breed mum-ed, shaking his fist up and down as he approached larcus.

"Still haven't got the hang of that boy, have you, aco?" Marcus said with a sly grin.

"I ain't feeding him no more, that's for damn sure," said, still disturbed over what had apparently ppened to him.

"Bit you again?"

"Hell, yes! Got my trigger finger, can you imagine?"

"You keep giving him a whack alongside the head d maybe one of these days he'll learn his place," arcus said, still smiling at the half-breed's misfor-ne.

"Oh, I did that, all right. Bloodied his nose a mite, I d. I'd gauge his food'll be cold once he comes to."

"Good." Discipline was one thing Monroe Marcus d always demanded in his camp.

Still shaking his finger, Paco said, "What I want to

know is, if I can't use my gun, what in the hell am gonna do in case of an emergency, Colonel?"

Again Marcus chuckled. "Tell you what, Paco, yo use that old saber you keep. Anyone gets close enoug to you, why, you oughtta be able to kill him fai enough."

The half-breed nodded agreement. "Not a bad idea Colonel. Send someone else to watch the boy while go get it."

Chance, Manuel, and one of the Kickapoo's bes trackers lay a hundred yards from the edge o Marcus's camp when Paco had taken a plate of food t Pepe and the boy had eagerly bitten him for hi efforts. It was nearing sunset and wouldn't be lon before they wouldn't be able to see the entire camp fo lack of light. Although Chance would never admit it, i had pained him to see the young lad cuffed across th face the way the half-breed had done. Still, it wa Manuel who had almost given them away.

"No!" Chance had growled when the Mexican despite his aching side, had nearly jumped to his fee and charged the camp all alone. However, he hadn' gotten but a foot off the ground when Chance ha placed a firm strong hand on Manuel's shoulder an planted him back on the ground between himself an the Kickapoo, who was also giving the Mexican harsh look.

"But Pepe—" Manuel pleaded, his face in pain a much for the suffering he saw on his nephew's face a for what he felt in his own side.

"I know, Manuel," Chance whispered. "But thi ain't the time or place. If we do this right, we'll get hir back tomorrow morning."

Chance had seen all he wanted to see of the cam

nd the men in it. He nodded toward the rear and the
Kickapoo caught his intent and the three of them
lowly crept back out of sight, to their horses. He
ould tell that Manuel, now out of breath and in pain,
vas quite disturbed over what he had just seen.

"You are sure? Tomorrow morning, for sure?" the
Mexican asked, barely able to mouth the words. The
nly thing that got them out, Chance thought, was the
vorry the man had for Pepe.

"That's right, old hoss. Tomorrow." Somehow,
Chance wished he could summon up the words to give
is man the confidence he knew he needed. Too bad
Vash wasn't here, he was always a lot better at things
ke this than Chance had ever been.

Mounted, he waited for Manuel to slowly climb
ito the saddle, a grimace of pain about him as he did.
In what he felt sure was a clumsy manner, Chance
niled and said, "You know, Manuel, that boy sure is
isty. I reckon his kind is worth saving any day of the
eek."

Despite the pain he was feeling, Manuel managed a
oad smile as he looked back at Chance and, with a
ood deal of pride, said, "That he is, my friend. That
is."

CHAPTER ★ 19 ★

Chance and Dallas were up long after the sun se
powwowing with the chief of the Kickapoo. Chanc
explained what he and Manuel and the warrior wh
had accompanied them had seen, doing his best t
persuade Chief Papequah that they would serve on
another's needs best if they worked together for a
least this one raid.

"I know you ain't got no love for us Texican
chief," he said, playing his final ace, "but I've got t
tell you that I don't recall ever warring on no Kicka
poo that I can remember. Mostly it's those damne
Comanches and then some of the Apaches out west b
the Pecos that I've spent my time in Texas fightin
with, at least as far as Indians go." He glanced

Dallas, who was listening intently since he would be doing the translating, wanting to get every word and phrase right. "Can't be much more truthful than that."

Dallas translated, once again using the sign language so popular among the frontier tribes. When it seemed that Chance's words had fallen on deaf ears, a frown formed on Dallas's face and he thought for a minute. "Chief, didn't you tell me that Pecan and some others of your tribal chiefs had made an agreement with the Mexican government to keep the Comanches and Apaches in the Coahuila district at bay?" The old mountain man spoke as he translated so Chance could hear his words, too. When Chief Papequah nodded, he added, "Well, from what my partner says, they's a couple Apaches in this group we're a-fighting. And, hell, comancheros is the same as Comanches in my book, and that's what the rest of these mangy critters is. Were it me, now, I'd help wipe out these uglies and find me the *jefe* of the *federales* in this territory and see couldn't I make me a deal with him 'bout keeping the Comanches and Apaches out of this land hereabouts. What do you think?"

The Kickapoo chief was thoughtful for a minute or two before signaling back his reply to Dallas. The mountain man turned to Chance and said, "He ain't so sure he could keep any kind of body at bay hereabouts. Remember what he said about not having ammunition for his repeater rifles?"

"Yeah." Chance nodded. "It does tend to put a limp in your style when all you've got is a lot of talk that ain't much more than bluff."

"Dealing in lead gets that way, I reckon."

"Tell him he can have those extra rifles of ours an
what ammunition we've got for 'em," Chance sai
after a brief moment of thought. "Tell him he ca
have everything in the camp we strike tomorrow. Hel
the only thing we come for was Pepe and maybe th
hide of that sorry-ass Marcus fella."

"Now you've got the idea," Dallas said with a smil
and turned to the chief. When he was through, an
seeing the chief would need at least a few minutes t
ponder the proposition, Dallas looked at Chance an
said, "I told him we'd spread the word far and wide o
how dangerous he and his men are."

When Chief Papequah spoke next, he still hadn
made a complete decision. "Got him the worries no
on whether the rifles we're passing on to him is gonn
be enough firepower for taking on this bunch
mangies."

A look of frustration crossed Chance's face, for h
wasn't used to being this picky about going off to wa
In his book, you simply checked your loads, saddle
up, rode square into their camp, and gave them hel
"If any of them repeater rifles he's got are Henry
or Spencers, he'll have plenty of reloads for 'en
along with the rifles we're giving him," he said wit
a frown.

"I'll make sure he knows that," Dallas said with
nod.

"You tell him one other thing, Dallas."

"What's that?"

"Tell him Grandpa said it ain't what you've got bu
how you use it," Chance grumbled, staring at the chi
as he spoke.

It didn't take Chief Papequah but a minute to agre
to have the better share of his warriors outside
Monroe Marcus's camp an hour before dawn.

Even an Indian knows when he's being challenged to fish or cut bait.

Sleep was minimal that night, if nonexistent. Chance and Dallas cleaned their own guns before going over the extra rifles they were going to hand over o the Kickapoo. They also made sure the weapons were fully loaded. Only after they were sure all they ad to do was strap on their guns and saddle and ide into battle did they settle in for a few hours of leep.

Ike Hadley and Manuel had turned in long before Chance and the mountain man. Chance figured the oy was likely wanting to get his beauty sleep. But lthough the Mexican turned in, Chance wasn't all hat sure he got much sleep that night. Not if the vorried look he'd carried around with him since hey'd returned from Marcus's camp that night was ny indication. Oh, Manuel was lying there on his ack with his sombrero pulled down over his face, but Chance had a sneaking suspicion that he was wide wake—worried about getting Pepe out all right, most kely. Not that a body could blame him. Hell, the lad as his nephew, wasn't he?

To his surprise, it was Ike Hadley who woke Chance arly the following morning. He also woke up Dallas nd Manuel, both of whom grumbled, for it was still itch dark. The four of them had fast cups of coffee hile they waited for Chief Papequah and the twenty so warriors who would be accompanying him on is raid.

If being awakened by a young man he considered zy at best was a surprise, Chance really had a umbfounded look about him when Ike disappeared d soon returned with the horses for all four of them,

as well as the extra one, which they all expected t
leave the enemy camp with Pepe riding it.

"Well, I'll be . . . saddled and all," Chance said i
what was little more than an amazed whisper. "Yo
trying to get on my good side, boy, or what?"

"I took Dallas to heart on the trail a while bac
Chance," was Ike's reply. "I don't figure you got n
good side. Now, what say we go see what kind of
storyteller you are?"

Chance wasn't sure whether the boy was trying t
pick a fight or just strutting his manhood. One thin
was sure—he had spunk, for he sounded as though h
meant every word he said. And that was a chang
from the loudmouthed lad who'd originally starte
out with them.

The ride Chance and Manuel had made out t
Marcus's camp had been a fruitful one. If nothin
else, he had been able to verify the truth of Chi
Papequah's estimate of Monroe Marcus and h
strength as a fighting unit. He'd counted upwards of
dozen men, most of them heavily armed with revol-
ers, knives, rifles, and bandoleers.

They knew the Marcus camp was only ten mil
from the Kickapoo lodges, so the amount of time
would take them to ride to the enemy camp was
given. The Kickapoo chief, Chance, and Dallas ha
sat around the fire going over a plan of attack, Chan
and Dallas mostly cleaning their weapons as the
listened to the chief and his idea for a plan of attac
And it wasn't half bad.

Papequah related a story to them that related
tactic he gauged to be similar to the one he would u
the next day. It seemed that several years ago, whe
the Kickapoo had known they were outnumbere
they had three of their men ride up to the enen

camp. Once the enemy knew they were there, a good share of them quickly saddled their horses and began to chase the three lone braves.

"Well, what happened?" an anxious Chance asked when the chief fell to silence. This Indian chief was nearly as good as his pa for working the suspense out of a tale.

Dallas translated Chance's words, then, after a brief exchange, smiled to himself as he turned back to Chance. "Says ary he tells you, his tactics won't be no good no more. Says to tell you he's telling the story and that should suffice."

Chance was still wondering about it as they left the Kickapoo camp that morning. All he and Dallas had been able to worm out of the chief was that the Kickapoo would position themselves at the eastern edge of the Marcus camp, while Chance and the rest would sneak up on the south side of the camp, free Pepe, and make a run for it. Chief Papequah felt confident about taking care of the rest. It somehow worried Chance and he found himself deep in concern about whether he would survive this morning's events. Was Rachel right? Would he someday never return from these daredevil adventures he continually found himself on? Would this be the one? Thank God it was still dark and no one could see the sweat that poured down his forehead and his back.

Strange as it seemed, he found himself trying to recall the prayers his mother had taught him as a child. Would they do him any good now? he wondered.

The Kickapoo left them a good half hour before dawn to take up their positions. Chance still found himself wondering what it was they had in mind. The four of them left their horses in a draw a mile from the

Marcus camp. It was the same place he and Manue had left their mounts the night before, so he had n trouble guiding the others up to the south side c camp.

Manuel placed a firm hand on his wrist and stoppe him in his tracks when they were only halfway to th camp. "It is I who must free Pepe, señor," he said in cautious whisper. His hand covered his mouth and h coughed slightly, spitting out a substance that seeme black in the dull morning gray.

"Why you?" Chance whispered back.

"It is I who am responsible for the boy's fate," th Mexican said in an adamant tone. "It is I who mu save him."

"Then the glory's all yours, hoss. Just don't tr being no hero until the chief gets his little war part going," Chance said with a half grin.

Chance gave a quick look at all three of h *compadres,* checking them out to make sure they ha everything they would need this morning. His gaz stopped on Ike Hadley and soon turned into a frow "Where's your goddamn rifle, boy?" he grumbled i an irritating whisper.

Ike shrugged, not particularly worried about i "Don't need no rifle, Chance. This is gonna b short-range shooting to be sure."

Chance looked about in the semidarkness, grabbe up a rather thin-looking branch of dead wood, an stuck it in Ike's hand. Shaking his head in disbelief, h said angrily, "And I had hopes for you."

The light of the morning sun had just begun t show, giving off just enough of a trace of dawn so th a man could see where he was going. And that looke like just what one of the comancheros was doing as h struggled down a path toward Pepe, who was sti bound to a tree, much as Chance and Manuel had seen him the night before.

The camp was only half awake when two braves came riding toward them, yelling at the top of their lungs. Bold as could be, they rode right up to the string of horses near camp, then wheeled their ponies to the rear and rode, racing, back to where they had come from. It got everyone's attention in camp, half asleep as they might be.

"June! Git the horses! Git after 'em! We'll teach the goddamn savages a lesson," Monroe Marcus said with a curse as he pulled one suspender over his shoulder. Within a minute half a dozen men were armed and mounted and chasing the renegade warriors.

"Now," Chance whispered to Manuel, next to him. But when he looked down, Manuel wasn't there.

As soon as the Indian ponies had spun to their rear, Manuel was on his feet and walking into camp. It didn't matter that he coughed and spit blood now—didn't matter at all. He had a knife in one hand and a six-gun in the other as he walked into camp, headed straight for Pepe, standing tall and proud as could be.

The Indians had everyone's attention in camp, including the big ugly who held a plate of beans for Pepe. Manuel felt a glow of pride within him as his nephew spit at the man, hitting him in the back with a big gob of spit. It was almost as though he had been saving that one gob of spit all night just for this moment. It caught the attention of the outlaw, who now turned and began to raise a fist as though to hit the boy.

"Please do not do that, señor," Manuel said in his politest tone of voice. It didn't seem to bother him that the man was twice his size and also had a knife and a gun, although both were sheathed and holstered.

"What! Who the hell are you?" the outlaw snarled suddenly dropping the plate of beans.

"Untie the young man before you and I will let yo live." Still occasionally spitting blood, Manuel didn' seem scared now at all. Perhaps the proof of this wa in the eyes of Pepe, who was looking over his shoul der, his eyes agog at the courage of his uncle, a courag he had never seen before.

"You're crazy," was all the outlaw said as he wen for his six-gun. Manuel shot him in the middle of th chest and the big man sank to the ground, dead.

"Quickly," Manuel said, bending down with th knife and cutting the boy's ties off both hands an feet. The boy was on his feet and in his arms, huggin him, but Manuel knew there was no time for that "The horses are in the ravine to the south," he added "You must go now."

"But—"

"Now, Pepe." There was authority in his voice an the boy knew it. He turned and ran as fast as he could

Chance, Dallas, and Ike all came up over the rise a soon as they heard Manuel's gunshot. All three stoo in awe as they saw the outlaw before the smallis Mexican fall to the ground in death. Dallas and Ik split up, each taking one side of the camp. Chanc walked right into camp as though the place were hi own.

No sooner had Manuel seen his nephew scampe down the slope toward the horses than he turned t confront a man who was almost bigger than the firs he had faced. But he didn't have a chance with thi man, for the outlaw stuck a big bowie knife in th Mexican's stomach as soon as he turned to face him Now the surprise was all Manuel's as the big ma turned the knife in his stomach, making sure he would die a painful death. Chance couldn't imagine the pain Manuel must be feeling as he saw the look on his face. But somehow he knew it didn't matter to the little Mexican anymore, as Manuel lifted his six-gun up into his attacker's side and pulled the trigger. The shot seemed to lift the man up into the air a ways before he fell back to the ground. With a look of disbelief of his own, he fell backward, dead.

Chance took two long strides toward Manuel, who was falling beside the second man he had killed, then stopped in his tracks and shot a third man headed their way. He, too, died a quick death. Whether he survived the day or not, Chance Carston was out for business when it came to dealing in lead.

One of the men who had gotten dressed faster than the rest had also headed for his horse. He might be a good man with a gun, but he knew when the firepower was more than he could stand. He had just mounted his horse and wheeled it to the right when Dallas shot him out of the saddle and muttered, "Sorry ass."

Ike had charged the camp, feeling kind of foolish with the piece of dead wood in his hand. Still, who was to say, maybe it would come in handy. It didn't. The first man he ran into was Paco, still lying in his blankets. But when he saw Ike standing over him, Paco was suddenly full of life. He pulled out the cavalry saber, just like Marcus had told him to, and waved it back and forth in front of him for protection. His first slice cut Ike's piece of dead wood in half, the second doing the same again. In utter surprise, Ike glanced at his dead wood, which was now simply a piece of kindling, mumbled, "To hell with that," drew his six-gun, and shot and killed Paco where he lay.

Chance had really taken a liking to Manuel an
knelt down beside him now that he'd killed the thir
man who had come their way. He was about to tak
the dying man in his arms when he heard anothe
nearby gunshot. When he looked up he saw ye
another man fall not ten feet from him. To his righ
stood Ike Hadley, his gun at holster level and smok
ing, looking as confident as he had a right to.

"How's that for one shot?" the lad asked.

"Like I said, there may be hope for you yet," wa
Chance's reply.

"I hope you make up your mind someday."

The shooting in camp died down and Chance too
the time to cradle Manuel in his arms.

"You'll be a real hero to that boy, amigo," he sai

The Mexican forced a smile. *"Sí.* It is importa
that a boy have his heroes, is it not?"

"I wonder if it ain't just as important that he kno
some love along the way," Chance said.

"But—"

"You showed him both, I think, amigo. Especiall
today."

Manuel coughed, spit some blood out the side of h
mouth, and gave Chance a genuine smile. "Yes, I di
didn't I?" It seemed to please him and Chance wa
glad for it as Manuel died.

"He's been spitting blood the last day or two," Ik
said, reloading his six-gun. "Made me promise I'
never tell you or Dallas about it. Think that's why h
wanted to go first? 'Cause he knew he was dying?"

"No, kid. I think he'd just gotten to believe i
himself again and found out how lonesome it can be.
think he was wanting someone else to believe in hin
too. Now they will."

"They?" Ike asked, confused.
"José and Rosa. That's who he did this for."

At least half of Marcus's men had climbed in the
addle to chase the Kickapoo who had charged their
amp and then, strangely, turned tail and run. It was
s though the Indians had suddenly caught a glimpse
f the size of the camp and the men in it and decided
hat this wasn't a day to raid for horses after all.
Vhatever the reason was, the sight of them fleeing had
aspired Marcus's men to give chase.
"Come on, boys, let's get 'em!" a man called Bones
ad yelled as he snapped a shot at one of them, even
hough the escaping warriors were well out of range.
aspired by Bones, the rest dug their heels into the
des of their mounts and pursued with a good deal of
elight. After all, they hadn't really had any fun with a
d savage for some time now.
They rode after the Indians, paired in twos, and
at was fine with Chief Papequah and his warriors as
ey lay in wait. Marcus's men had ridden hard for
arly half a mile when it seemed as though the Indian
onies were slowing down, losing speed for some
ason or another. Whatever it was, it gave the Marcus
oup that much more desire to catch up with the
uding Kickapoo. They were so excited, in fact, that
didn't even cross their minds that they were about
use up all six shots in their six-guns. Truth be told,
didn't come to them until they were almost upon
e Kickapoo riders. It was then they heard the distant
nfire in their own camp.
It was then they knew, one and all, that they had
dden into a trap.
Upwards of fifteen Kickapoo warriors suddenly

appeared on either side of them. It was as though the
were part of the scenery, of the plains, and had quietl
and quickly materialized out of nowhere. The tw
men in the lead were shot out of the saddle by two c
Chief Papequah's best shots. The warriors who di
the shooting quickly seized hold of the dead men'
horses before they could get away.

The third rider used his last shot to kill the Kicka
poo who came after him. However, he was soon kille
by a lengthy spear from the warrior who replaced hin
His partner was not so lucky, having already used u
his six shots. The warrior he had aimed at grabbe
him by the arm with one strong hand, yanked him ou
of the saddle, and slit his throat with his knife befor
the outlaw hit the ground.

The last two riders had reined in their mount
knowing that they had lost their riding partners to th
trap. They tried their best to turn about and flee thes
attackers but it was too late for them, too. One of th
riders was shot out of the saddle by another of th
Kickapoo riflemen, for Papequah had anticipated th
actions of these men.

The last rider was surprised to see what looked lik
an ancient old man charging at him. The old man, a
of seventy-five, carried with him what had once been
Sharps rifle. But the stock was now gone, broken off i
combats of the past. All he had left now was the heav
long barrel of the rifle and it would do what he desire
of it. He swung it at the rider, whose horse ha
whinnied and nearly bucked its rider out of th
saddle, completing the job the horse started by knock
ing the last man off his mount. The warrior then bega
to mercilessly beat his enemy to death, rememberin
all too well the white man who had killed his wife s
many years ago.

Within five minutes of the time they had ridden nto the trap, half of the men of Marcus's band were lead.

Back at the camp of Monroe Marcus, Chance and Dallas walked among the dead men, looking for one who was tall and lean and matched the description hat José Quesada had given them. There were several all, heavyset men, but none to match the look or the arb of Monroe Marcus.

"Son of a bitch," Chance muttered to himself, ngry at having let the chief honcho get away.

"You thinking what I'm thinking?" Dallas asked.

Chance nodded. "Gutless bastard rode off and left is men to die for him."

"Sounds like you better climb on that horse of yours nd head out after him, Chance," Ike Hadley said. To Chance's surprise, Ike sounded like he was one of hem, sounded as though he knew what was on Chance's mind.

"Dallas—" Chance started to say, but was interupted by Ike.

"Don't you worry none about this mess, Chance. Me and Dallas will clean it up."

"The lad's right, son. You catch up with this cowd, you do him right, you hear? We'll catch up with ou at José's place," Dallas said with conviction.

"Thanks," he said to both of them, then ran like hell ack to the draw and his horse.

He hadn't counted on meeting Pepe, who was aiting by the horses, just as his uncle had told him to .

"Is Manuel up there?" the boy asked. "Is he in the mp?"

Chance gave the boy a heartfelt look, but knew he

didn't have the time to explain to him what ha
happened to his uncle. He had an outlaw to catch
"Yeah, Pepe, he's up there."

Once Chance had mounted up, he was about to pul
the reins when he stopped. "Pepe?"

"Yes, sir."

"You got you an uncle who's a real hero now, yo
understand?" he said.

The boy's face broke out in a wide grin. "Yes,
know."

"Good. Don't you ever forget it."

Then he was gone, tracking down one last outla
from this group of misfits. And that man was Monro
Marcus.

CHAPTER

★ 20 ★

[illegible]elp me up, woman. Today I will take my coffee and [illegible]eals at the table, like a man should," José said from [illegible]s bed as he watched Rosa prepare his morning meal. [illegible]e had been in bed nearly a week now and found that [illegible] disliked it very much. Even if it hurt, he knew that [illegible]man must be a man. And although Rosa was a loving [illegible]other and wife, in the back of his mind José [illegible]spected that she secretly felt he might become lazy if [illegible] were to stay in bed any longer. So today, even [illegible]ough his side still hurt, he had made the decision to [illegible]alk like a man once more.

Rosa helped José out of bed in silence, handing him [illegible]homemade crutch she had fashioned after his beat[illegible]g. It was a sturdy piece of work but helped José only

slightly. Once José had made it to the table an
awkwardly seated himself, she brought his plate t
him, nearly slammed it on the table before him, an
uttered, "Men!" in a rather disgusted tone.

There was much work to do and only Maria to hel
her with it now that Pepe was gone. She spent th
morning out back washing clothes. There were onl
the clothes for herself and her daughter to do now, an
they were few. The day Chance Carston and hi
friends had left she had washed Pepe's clothes, know
ing that she would never have to wash them agai
until he safely returned. But whether the big Amer
can who called himself their friend would ever be abl
to bring back her son, she did not know. So she ha
washed the boy's clothes and placed them on his be
where she determined they would stay until he wa
returned to her.

It was approaching the noon hour when she heard
horse riding toward the house. One quick look out th
front window struck terror in her heart and sh
quickly left the kitchen area for the backyard. "Mari
Quick! The root cellar! The *norteamericano* is here!
In bug-eyed silence, Maria made her way into the ro
cellar in no time flat.

Monroe Marcus didn't bother to knock. He simpl
kicked the door in and stood in the doorway, bigg
than life, trying to adjust his eyes to the darkne
inside the adobe structure.

"I would ask you to sit but I fear you will not sta
long," José said in as calm a voice as ever. He was sti
seated at the kitchen table, where he had spent most
the morning.

"Shut up, old-timer," Marcus growled. "I need gru
for a long trip and I need it now. Come on, where

hat bitch you're married to?" He took a step inside, still waiting for his eyes to adjust properly.

When Rosa had gotten her daughter hidden safely away, she had ducked in the back door and found a dark shadow to stand in. She had given this situation much thought and had determined to be prepared for it if indeed it did take place. She had it all planned, knew exactly what she would do.

"I am right here, señor," she said, and stepped into the edge of the shadow where, even if he had already adjusted his eyes, he could barely see her. "But you will not bully us anymore."

Puzzled, Marcus glanced at José for an answer. "What the hell's she talking about, old man?"

"I would not take her lightly, señor. She is a woman of determination, my Rosa," was all José would say.

"I do not like you, Señor Marcus. You beat my husband and take our food and make my son a hostage," Rosa said in an even tone. She stepped out of the shadows so he could plainly see the shotgun she held close to her side. She cocked both barrels and said, "You are an evil man and there is no place for you in this world. You must go and go now."

Monroe Marcus gave José a confused look, as though he couldn't believe the bold words he was hearing. But José's only reply came in the form of a mischievous grin, which made Marcus mad as hell.

"The hell you say," Marcus growled, and went for his gun.

Rosa pulled the trigger of the shotgun. The sound inside the home was deafening to say the least. It knocked Rosa back, but knocked Monroe Marcus back even further. The buckshot tore a hole in his stomach as he slammed back into the side of the doorway. His legs lost all of their strength and he slid down into a sitting position, staring in astonishment at the woman and the shotgun she held. He died shaking his head back and forth in disbelief.

When Rosa looked up, she saw Chance Carston standing in the doorway next to the body of Monroe Marcus. He had a six-gun in his hand but it was obvious he hadn't fired it.

"Told you you'd be good with that shotgun," was all he said, and gave her a wink and a nod.

Realizing what she had just done, the death she had brought upon this man, she dropped the shotgun and rushed into Chance's arms, crying.

José had no objections. "I told him she was woman of determination," he said with a shrug.

"So it would seem," Chance said, still holding the crying woman in his arms.

CHAPTER

★ 21 ★

Rosa found him out back near a cottonwood tree
Iaria often played about. He had found a spade in
ıe barn and begun to dig what looked like a grave. It
as the middle of the afternoon and the heat had
ecome unbearable, even for those who were used to
ving in such a climate. When he looked up, she
anded him a glass of cool water. He took it gratefully,
imbing out of the hole and heading for the shade of
e cottonwood.

"Surely you do not intend to bury the *bandido* back
ere," she said to Chance. "It is here that we intend
ır own loved ones to be buried when they pass on."

"I know. It's what Maria told me earlier." Chance
ıished the water and handed the glass back to her.
ith a half smile he said, "Mighty nice flower garden

you got there next to the barn. Ain't that where planted them plug-uglies the last time I was here?"

"Sí," she said with a nod, returning the smile. " remember José telling me about it." Chance remem bered it well, too. He had stripped the outlaws wh had died at the Quesada residence and dug a mas grave for them, assuring José that their bodies wer the same as manure. The decomposed bodies woul produce a fine crop of whatever José planted atop th grave.

"I got Monroe Marcus laid out over by that ga den," Chance said, trying to be reassuring in his ton "I'll be planting him same as I did those others whe I'm through here."

At first Rosa let out a sigh of relief, but it was soo followed by a look of distress as she realized that th grave Chance was now digging could only be for member of her family. A hand went up to her mout as though to hide the quiver of her lips. Chance kne she was crying again. He also knew why and was soo on his feet, placing a big, strong arm about he shoulder to comfort her.

"It ain't what you're thinking, you know." H thought he heard the whimper stop as Rosa looked u at him, confused.

"But—"

"Pepe's fine," he said with a smile. "Got a lot c spunk, that boy does."

"And Manuel?"

"I reckon he felt it was his fault the boy got taken i the first place. But I'll tell you one thing, Rosa. H wasn't nowhere close to lacking courage," Chanc said in a more serious tone. "Walked right into cam bold as day. Shot the guard standing over Pepe and c the boy's bonds in no more than five seconds.

Chance wanted this woman to know that her brother had died a genuine hero. "Pepe—he knows his uncle was a real hero that day. And I don't think he'll soon forget it."

"Good. I am glad for that," she said in a sad way.

Slowly, she turned to walk back to the house. She had only taken a few steps when Chance's voice stopped her.

"Rosa?"

"Sí," she said when she turned back to him.

"Just between you and me, he'd been spitting blood those last couple of days. Can't say for sure, but I think one of his ribs busted from all that riding and punctured one of his lungs," he said. "Doctor I know back in Twin Rifles told me once things like that happen."

"Then he knew he was dying," she said.

"Don't make him any less a hero in that boy's eyes," Chance said. Then, remembering the dying man's words, he added, "I reckon everyone's got to have a hero."

Then the strangest thing happened. Rosa silently walked up to him, pulled his face down to her, and softly kissed him on the lips. Before their lips had parted, Chance knew he was turning a fiery shade of red in the face.

"Now, what in the devil was that for?" he asked, amazed.

There was a hint of a smile about her, the kind he had seen on Rachel every once in a while, as she said, "Yes, everyone must have his hero."

Then she headed back toward the adobe structure. And Chance, for the life of him, couldn't figure out what in the hell had just taken place.

CHAPTER

★ 22 ★

Dallas and Ike showed up just before sunset that da
Chance had dug the grave deep enough and wa
working at putting together a coffin of sorts when the
rode into the yard.

"Looks like you could use a hand," Dallas offere
when he spotted Chance just outside the barn. Wit
out so much as a greeting, Ike Hadley had silent
taken the horses off to be watered and curried. The
had put in a good day's work keeping up with Chan
and trying to get to the Quesada residence.

As for Pepe, he had slid off his mount as fast
anyone could ever recall seeing him move and quick
made his way inside, running into his mother's arn
at the door. The woman had held on to him as thoug
he were life itself, and perhaps in a way he was. B

:hat is usually the way of a mother. Maria had even ;iven her brother a hug. It was José who had told the ɔoy to sit down at the table and tell him all about his ıdventure, for by now that was what it had become. ⁴nd just as Chance had promised, Pepe painted his ıncle to be quite the hero of the whole affair. When he old of how Manuel had died, José and Rosa were lutifully sad and proud at the same time. It was as hough Chance had never uttered a word about Manuel's actions and deeds.

"That boy still trying to get on my good side?" Chance asked as Dallas helped with the making of the offin.

The old mountain man glanced at Ike and grinned ɔ himself. "I don't know who it is he's a-trying to npress, but he sure has taken on one whole lot of esponsibility these last couple of days. Why, shoot, ou should have seen him, taking after them horses ke they was his own and treating the boy like he was ne of us." Dallas shook his head in a bit of disbelief. No, he ain't no flannelmouth no more. That's for ıre."

It was dark by the time their crudely fashioned ɔffin was ready for use, but José and Rosa agreed that was best to hold their own little ceremony now and t it over with. They would get a hold of the mission ıdre and have him bless the grave site when they uld. José, leaning on his homemade crutch, toted s Bible up to the grave and read from a favorite rse of his as they laid Manuel to rest.

While the older Mexican read from the Good Book, hance's mind was on Rachel and how much he issed her. He had done his best to keep her out of his ind when they had run into the Kickapoo and then ıring the fight with Marcus and his men, but now

that it was all over he found himself consumed witl
the thought of her. At first he wasn't sure why, bu
then it crossed his mind that he actually did love he

Was it indeed time to settle down, like Wash ha
done with Sarah Ann? Perhaps so. Hell, he wasn'
getting any younger. And he liked the horse-breakin
business that he and his brother were in, wouldn'
mind doing it as long as his bones didn't go bad o
him. Not that it wasn't dangerous, mind you. It wa
just that these little adventures that he wound u
getting into, why, they usually turned out to be a lo
more dangerous than breaking any wild mustan
could ever be.

The whole thing—thinking about Rachel and all—
gave him a warm feeling that he hadn't experience
for some time now. When was it—the last time he wa
on one of these expeditions? Yeah, that was it. The
he felt a sudden cold chill run down his spine as h
realized that it could have been him they were buryin
now and not Manuel. Was Rachel right in her fear tha
someday he wouldn't return? Was this that one time
After all, he wasn't back within the city limits of Twi
Rifles yet. What if something else were to happen
What if . . . ?

Afterward, in the darkness of evening, Chanc
steered Ike Hadley aside to the corral, where th
moonlight gave off the only light.

"Dallas says you been doing right well, helping hi
and the boy out on the trip back here," he said in
relatively soft tone of voice.

"I been trying."

There was silence as the two stood there and looke
out over the corral into the night.

"I wanted to thank you for saving my life the oth
day," Chance said softly, looking into the distance

ıe spoke. It was about as humble as anyone would ver see or hear him get.

Ike Hadley had a chance to shove it all down this nan's throat if he cared to. But perhaps Dallas was ight and he had grown some into manhood. One hing was sure—no matter how he might have felt bout Chance Carston, Ike Hadley knew that you took man's thanks when you could get them, for they vere few and far between. Especially when the subject vas the saving of one's life.

"As I recall, most of the talking that day was being one by our guns," he said in an even tone. "Humans idn't have much say about it."

"Still, I wanted to thank you for—"

"De nada, amigo. I figure you'd have done the same or me," Ike said as though it were nothing. They were ıe kind of words a man put a great deal of stock in, or they were usually spoken to you by a friend. And ven for a man who was as much a loner as Chance arston, they were words that he appreciated, for he new the man next to him meant them.

"One thing about them grave diggers, kid," Chance ıid with a stretch of the arms.

"What's that?" Ike asked.

"They sure do sleep well. Me—I'm turning in."

CHAPTER ★ 23 ★

Charlie and Ethan Wade had been sitting in Wi
Carston's jail for upwards of two weeks now. The
were being held for attempted bank robbery. A
tempted, hell! They'd had the money in the flour sack
and were nearly on their horses when the marshal an
a stubborn-looking farmer named Emmett had gotte
the drop on them and paraded them off to the cell the
now occupied. Be that as it may, the two men consi
ered themselves to be plenty tough and had more tha
one scar apiece to prove it. It was just that Ethan ha
all of his scars on his face and thus looked uglier tha
sin on Sunday. And Charlie would never let him forg
it.

"Oh, shut up your goddamn mouth," Ethan be

owed as Charlie once again made a cutting remark bout his brother's looks.

"And I suppose you're gonna make me, huh?" was Charlie's reply. One would have thought the two of hem were no more than five years old the way they quabbled among themselves.

The door connecting the cells with the marshal's ffice opened and Joshua Holly stomped down the all, looking frustrated as could be. "Now you listen ere," he growled, shaking a piece of wood he'd been hittling on at the two men behind bars. "You mangy ırs just shut your mouths, the both of you, or I'll take ıat bowie knife of mine and do some whittling on ɔu critters instead of this dead wood. Now just shut p, hear?"

The Wade brothers, for all their constant bickering, ıd yet to get used to the middle-aged deputy and his ıreats. They had decided that he had absolutely no nse of humor, which was not true at all. Joshua olly simply refused to put up with riffraff like the 'ade brothers. However, the deputy had convinced e two prisoners that he had no humor when, that st week, they had screamed and yelled at one ıother childishly. The first time the deputy had ırged through the door to the marshal's office, he had ven them fair warning. It was what he had done the cond time, when they had ignored his warning. shua had charged in, keys in one hand, a madder-an-hell look about him. He had opened the cell or, wiggled a finger at Ethan to come hither, and ocked him clear across the room when the bank ɔber had approached him.

"I wouldn't laugh ary I was you, sonny," the deputy d growled at Charlie when the brother had snick-

ered at Ethan's ill fortune. "You do and you're likel
to wind up just as ugly as him and feeling worse, if
have anything to do with it."

Both Wade brothers had kept that encounter i
mind, swearing to one another that if they ever did g
out of this place, why, they would likely kill th
deputy just for the hell of it.

When Joshua Holly had gone back to his whittli
in the marshal's office, the brothers had little more t
do than sit across from one another and be bored.

"You don't think he'd really take a knife to us, d
you, Charlie?" Ethan asked after a while.

"I don't know, Ethan, but you'd think you'd be use
to it by now, what with all them scars you got on yo
face," was Charlie's reply.

Ethan was silently sitting there, mulling over th
prospect of perhaps killing his brother one of the
days if he didn't stop joshing him about his look
when he heard a foreign sound. He glanced at the ba
that crossed the one window they had to the outsi
world, then glanced back at Charlie.

Recognition seemed to come to both of them at th
same time and they rushed to the window bars.

"Well, I'll be damned," Ethan said with a look th
was filled with amazement.

"Most of us are, fool." The words came from Har
Aker, who was accompanied by his partner, Sa
Bayles.

"See, Charlie? I told you they'd come to get us, on
the word got out." Ethan seemed to feel his confiden
building within him again. Spending two weeks in
jail cell is not only a lonely proposition but tends to
hell on a man's spirits. "That is what you're here fo
ain't it? You did come to get us out of this rat ho

idn't you, Harry? Sam?" As quickly as his confi-
ence had built, it had been replaced by the fear of a
esperate man.

"You betcha, Ethan," Harry said with a playful
mile.

"Well, when's it gonna be?" Charlie asked anx-
ously.

Harry shrugged noncommittally. "A few more
ays. We're still looking over the town, you know."
arry wasn't about to tell his former gang members
at he was getting quite uncomfortable in Twin
ifles, especially with the near run-ins he had recently
ad with the law. It didn't pay to get all that well
nown in these small towns, particularly when you
ere there to do something like break some friends
ut of jail. Townsfolk—the lawmen in particular—
owned on it.

"Well, I hope you don't take too much long-
, Harry. Ethan here is getting downright ugly to
ve with," Charlie said with a chuckle at his own
ke.

"Yeah, I can see that," Harry replied to him, giving
f his own laugh. Ethan Wade wasn't having a good
y at all when it came to his looks.

"Quiet, Harry," Sam said with a frown. "We're
king a chance just being back here and talking to
ese two, you know." To the prisoners, he added,
Ve've got to git. We'll stop by again and let you know
at night we'll be pulling the breakout."

As though Sam's words were an omen, there was a
uder-than-usual noise on the boardwalk at the en-
nce of the alley.

A jittery Harry said, "What the hell was that?"

To which Sam replied, "I don't know. Looked like

that tinhorn carrying another of those trays back t
the eatery down the street."

Harry, now a mite worried, said, "Let's get the he
outta here."

Sam nodded agreement and they were gone almos
as soon as they had arrived.

Jeremiah Younger had been returning with a tra
full of empty plates. If having an appetite was any sig
that Carny Hadley was recovering, well, Carny Hadle
was recovering. He had enjoyed another pleasant tal
with Wilson Hadley and was considering whistling–
he felt that good—when he heard the raucous laugh o
Harry Aker. Jeremiah had stopped dead in his track
which just happened to be at the mouth of the alle
leading to the rear of the jail. He had swallowed har
not believing what he was hearing, and had eventuall
coughed loudly. It was then he had taken what he too
to be several normal steps past the alleyway. He'
stopped dead still once again and thought for
moment.

He returned the tray and empty plates to Margar
Ferris at the Ferris House, then dismissed himself fo
what he called "business" he had to take care of.

When he returned to the marshal's office, he near
bumped into Joshua as the deputy left to go to get
meal. Behind him, and seated at his big oak desk, wa
Will Carston, the law and order of Twin Rifles.

"Yes, sir, Mr. Younger, what can I do for you?" th
lawman asked with a smile almost as pleasant as tha
of Wilson Hadley.

"Well, Marshal, it's like th-this," a nervous Jerem
ah said with a stutter. "I know I've not been muc
good to your community, and I fully intend to b
moving on soon, but, ah . . ."

"Come on, man, spit it out," Will demanded as he rose to his feet.

"Marshal, do you mind if I come in and have a rather private talk with you? Perhaps I may be able to do your community some good after all."

"Have a seat, tinhorn," Will said. "And I'll have a listen."

CHAPTER

★ 24 ★

They got an early start the next morning. Chanc
Dallas, and Ike all knew that their mission had bee
accomplished. Pepe had been rescued and the likes c
Monroe Marcus would never be seen in this territor
again.

According to Dallas, Chief Papequah and his Kick
apoo would be considered heap big medicine now th
they had gotten rid of a group of comanchero raider
and the handful of Apache renegades who had accom
panied them on their foul deeds. "I convinced th
chief I'd talk him up to being right next in importanc
to those fire gods in the sky who control everything,
Dallas had said with a grin that was only half humo
ous. Chance knew that the old mountain man was bi
on saying what you mean and meaning what you sa

and succeeded more than most men when it came to living by his own words. He figured it was likely one reason the old-timer had lived as long as he had. So if Dallas Bodeen said he'd talk this Kickapoo chief up as some kind of hero, why, he'd do just that.

Ike Hadley had eaten a quick morning meal and quickly disappeared while Chance and Dallas said heir good-byes to José, Rosa, and the kids. And sure enough, when they walked out front, there was Ike with their horses saddled and ready to go.

Chance shook his head in disbelief and said, "I still ay—"

"Yeah, I know, I'm trying to get on your good side. Yeah, I know, Chance," Ike replied in what Chance hought to be a bit of a playful mood. "But I keep emembering what Dallas said, about you not having o good side."

For the first time in a long time, Chance smiled, and was directed at Ike Hadley. "Shut up, kid. We gotta it."

"Not until I say good-bye," the youth said, and alked over to Maria. For all the childish play the two f them had experienced, Ike Hadley saw much more this young girl's face than anyone else might. "I ally enjoyed your company, Miss Maria," he said, ddenly turning shy.

"And I yours, Señor Ike," she said with a blush and shy smile.

"Don't you be surprised if I make time to come ck this way in a couple of years, ma'am," Ike said to osa. "I got a notion your daughter is gonna turn into real beauty—just like her mama," he added with a ink and a smile.

Maria buried her face in her mother's shoulder to de the embarrassment she felt over being talked about as though she were some object. Or was i because she wasn't sure of her own feelings at th moment? She truly had developed a desirous feelin for young Ike Hadley, but at the same time she house a fear that she would never see him again—that h would simply move on and never return to see her.

"You will always be welcome here," Rosa said wit a grateful smile. "All of you."

"I believe the boy has an eye for beauty," José sai with a grin.

An unusually patient Chance said, "If you folks ar through with all them good-byes, we gotta git. There' a woman back in Twin Rifles who's worrying abou me more than she should."

They made a good deal of distance that day, espe cially in the morning hours, when it was still coo There were just the three of them now and they wer in relatively good health. There was no more haulin around dead bodies or escorting young lads who ha been captured and taken hostage—none of that foo ishness. Both Chance and Dallas had learned long ag that it is beneficial to watch your back trail. Thing always look different when you're going in the oppo site direction. They knew the trail back to Twin Rifle and remembered the water holes and how scarce c plentiful the water supply was at each. Mostly it wa scarce.

With their business done, Chance's thoughts drifte to Rachel as they rode that day. More and more, h was realizing how lucky he was to have a woman lik that set her cap for him. And the more he thought c it—the more he thought of Rachel—the more h came to realize that he couldn't save the whole worl Perhaps he had made too many promises to too mar people over the years, for just as in the case of José Quesada, they seemed to pop up every once in a while—people he'd promised his help to way back when and had nearly forgotten about by now. Still, when they reminded you of what you'd said, well, a man didn't break his word, that was for sure. So you went, just like he had gone this time.

Of course, he had almost gotten killed, too. The kid, Ike Hadley, had definitely saved his life back at the camp of Marcus and his renegades. Chance knew that he had broken one of his own rules; he'd gotten personally involved with someone, and it had nearly gotten him killed. He'd gotten to liking Manuel and maybe even caring about the man. It was that caring that had made him kneel down beside Manuel when the man was dying instead of charging on like a bull as he usually did. If the Hadley boy hadn't been there and shot that one last son of a bitch, Chance knew good and well he might not be here today. He just didn't want to make the same mistake with the boy, for he was now convinced that the lad had what it took to make a go of it in this land. The fact of the matter was that, although he'd never admit it to him, Chance kind of hoped Ike Hadley would make it back down to the Quesada spread and take up with that girl, Maria. He thought they'd make a nice pair.

It was during the afternoon of their second day of riding that all hell broke loose. Like the previous day, the trio had made great strides in their riding distance during the cool early hours of the morning. It was the afternoons, when it seemed the hottest to both man and beast, that they had slacked off and given the horses more resting time. The land was still flat, with occasional cottonwoods found around the water holes. And in the distance to the west could be seen

the tips of what Dallas thought to be the Serranía de
Burro mountain range as it stretched down int
Mexico. More than once, each man found himsel
wishing he were at the top of one of those mountai
peaks, for it would be considerably cooler and muc
more tolerable weatherwise. Chance was trying t
think of what he would say to Rachel on his return t
Twin Rifles when Dallas pulled his horse to a halt,
worried look about him.

"Uh-oh," he said in a tone that matched the expres
sion on his face. The words immediately brough
Chance out of his reverie.

"Damn," he muttered to himself, catching sight c
the riders in the distance. "I was hoping we could ge
by those pilgrims. Ain't much in the mood for fightin
now."

"Looks like mood ain't gonna have one whol
helluva lot to do with it, they get any closer," Ik
Hadley said as he saw the same thing Dallas an
Chance did.

They weren't much different than the first bunc
Chance recalled encountering on their way into Mex
co. Some of the riders were scrawny, just like th
leader of the last group, while some were fat. Ther
were even a handful of them who wore the uniform c
a *federal* soldier. Likely they had killed the men the
had originally belonged to. And they were well armec
brandishing six-guns, knives, and rifles as though the
were out hunting in full force. And, of course, the
were. But if he had had one, Chance would have bet
dollar that the lot of them were hired guns for tha
Juán Cortinas character, the warlord who seemed t
think he owned this part of Mexico and everyone in i

"What do you reckon, a dozen of 'em?" Chanc

ısked Dallas as he dismounted and opened one of his ;addlebags. Rummaging around inside, he pulled out ı Colt Army model .44. It was the one he'd used in the war as a cavalryman, and even after he'd managed to ;crounge a brand-new Colt conversion model, he'd kept the extra six-gun. It wasn't just for sentimental easons, either. He'd known it would come in handy omeday—like now. He checked the loads and shoved t in his pant waist.

"Lessen my eyes is failing me, I count a dozen, naybe a couple more," Dallas said. Seeing that the iders were still headed his way, he dismounted and ulled some extra shells from his pocket, loading his Ienry rifle to its fullest. He jacked a round in the hamber, ready for bear.

"Looks like that Marcus shoot-out all over again," ke said with a shake of his head. The only one who vas still mounted, he needed only to see the frown on Chance's face before adding, "But, hell, why miss the ighlight of my day?" Somehow he knew he had to ay, had to fight it out by their sides. Hell, he was one f them now, wasn't he?

Chance grabbed the reins of his horse and led the .ount away a short distance, swatting it on the rump ıd sending it off a ways.

Dallas did the same.

"What are you doing that for?" Ike asked.

"Don't want my horse getting shot," was Chance's ply. "I survive this mess, catching him up will be .sy as pie." He paused a moment and shrugged. "If ey kill me, it won't make a damn bit of difference ıyway, will it?"

"Reckon not," Ike said, and did the same with his ount.

"Odds is considerable worse than going up agains Marcus and his bunch," Dallas said as the warlord' riders closed on them.

"Something like five to one, I'd say," Chance saic

"Too bad we ain't got that chief and his Kickapoc We could sure use 'em now," Ike said, talking a though it would have a calming effect. But it didn' for his palms still felt sweaty. "I don't reckon praye would do much good, huh?"

"Well, son, I never was much of a churchgoer, but can remember more than one time I've called on m Maker in a pinch and He come through for me, Dallas said, all the time watching the riders com nearer and nearer.

"If you know any prayers, this would be the time t say 'em," Chance said. Like Dallas, he had his eyes o the riders he would soon confront, but in the back (his mind he was wondering if this would be the da that he'd die. For suddenly he had a desperate desi to live—a profound need to get back to Rachel, to se her just one more time. Chance Carston had nev been much of a churchgoer, either, but in a moment silence he found himself seeing if he could rememb how the "Our Father" was recited.

"Ah, you must be the ones," the leader of th warlords said when he'd managed to get his horse- and those of his crowd—all of five yards in front Chance, Dallas, and Ike. No one had drawn a gun ye so for the moment this was simply a friendly exchan about the state of the weather.

"Depends on who you're looking for, I reckon Chance said in an even tone. For once in his life was using a bit of tact, the kind Wash was alwa trying to tell him was better than a sure-enough figh

"Yes, you are the ones." The leader was of mediu

ɔuild, although it was hard telling sometimes when a nan was seated on his horse. A bit more muscular han the scrawny one had been. But just as pushy. He ;ave a confident smile as he added, *"Sí,* the old one, he big one, and the young one."

"Some might call us that, I reckon," Chance said. 'What's it to you? Hell, what's your name?"

"You will call me El Jefe." Used to having his way, e was. He squinted a moment, as though to find omething that should be there but wasn't. "Where is our friend, the scared one? The *mejicano?"*

"Buried him a couple of days back," Ike said in a trong voice. "But there wasn't nothing scared about im then. Fact is, he had half a dozen dead men at his ɛet by the time he died. I call that downright brave."

"You still didn't answer my question. What's your iterest in us?" Chance said, his voice a bit harder ow. He was sure he knew what the answer would be, ut he wanted to hear it from this man's mouth, anted to know for sure before the lead started flying.

It was then he noticed that the riders not directly in ont of him had begun to slowly sidestep their ounts until they formed two ranks of seven men ıch, side by side. They would have to go through the en in one rank to get to the man behind him. And hance had a notion that most of El Jefe's best ooters were lined up in that first row.

"Oh, that," El Jefe said with a crooked smile. "I am ı orders to find you."

"Seems like you accomplished that," Chance said. Now what?"

Two thoughts ran through his mind right then and ey were both confusing. The first one was that this fe, or chief honcho, or whatever he wanted to be own as, had a certain madness in his eyes. He had

come to complete a mission and they all knew wha
that was. The second thought was somewhat mythica
he figured. In the distance, past the rear of thes
warlords, he could have sworn he saw the flash c
sunlight off a piece of metal. Or was it a mirror? I
couldn't be the Kickapoo coming to save them, coul
it? No, they were two days' ride from here. Still, the
was that one glimmer of hope inside that prayed th
it was just that. That, after all, seemed about the onl
way the three of them would get out of this fix.

"Now I carry out the second part of my orders."

"Which are?"

"To kill you, of course."

The conversation sort of dried up about then as I
Jefe went for his six-gun. His actions were followed b
each and every one of his men. The afternoon erupte
in gunfire, more gunfire than Chance had thought he'
heard in quite some time, maybe even since the wa
He pulled his Colt and shot El Jefe and the man ne
to him out of their saddles. He took a step to the rig
and fired twice at the man behind El Jefe's no
skittish horse. The man took both slugs in the che
and fell from his horse, but not before he had fired h
own six-gun and hit Chance in the leg. But the soun
of gunfire and smell of gunsmoke had brought out th
mad in Chance Carston and he stubbornly refused t
fall, staggering a bit to hold his own, but standing ju
the same.

Dallas had quickly shot the front two riders out
their saddles and seemed purely amazed when h
jacked a third round into the chamber of his Hen
rifle but couldn't find a rider on either of the hors
behind the first two riders to shoot at. He darte
abruptly to his left and saw the two of them lying c
the ground, apparently lifeless. It baffled him that th

wo shots he had fired had gone directly through their argets and struck the rider behind them. But what lse could it be, he wondered?

To his surprise, young Ike Hadley didn't feel any ear at all when the shooting started. He pulled his ix-gun just as slick as you please and fired his shots ff as calmly as though he were shooting at paper argets. His first shot hit the man in front of him, earing open a vein in his neck that made him worry nore about bleeding to death than being shot to leath. Ike pulled the trigger a second time and hit his arget again, a big fat man who took the bullet in the tomach. But he was far from dead and had time to do ome shooting himself. Ike took the first bullet high in ne chest, knocking him backward a step but not utting him out of the fight at all. He knew he was urt but he also knew he had a fight to the death on his ands. Chance and Dallas were his friends and he ouldn't let them down. His third shot took one of the arlords in the head, killing him instantly as he fell om his horse, blood and brains falling down the side f his saddle as he fell to the ground. Ike took a second ullet square in the chest as he was bringing his x-gun up to aim at a man who was already falling out his saddle in a lifeless manner.

Then suddenly the gunfire stopped just as quickly as had started. And to the surprise of all of them, there asn't a one of El Jefe's riders left in the saddle. Each them—Dallas, Chance, and Ike—figured that one their partners had killed the rest of the ones they dn't gotten.

Still holding his Colt firmly in hand, Chance turned Ike, who was still standing but looking a mite aked, and said, "By God, Ike, you remind me of e."

Ike Hadley's face was almost pure white, as thoug
the blood had been drained from him, and judgin
from the holes in his chest, most of it had. But a
tough and stubborn as Chance, the boy had all bu
willed himself to remain standing—at least for now
He glanced over his shoulder at Chance and said
"You know, Chance, that's all I ever wanted to hear.
Then he dropped his gun and toppled to the groun
as dead as the rest about him.

Chance wanted to kneel down beside the boy in th
worst way, just like he had with Manuel, but he kne
that he must not, for there were more riders comin
toward them and God only knew if they were friendl
or wanting in on this fight.

The handful of riders turned out to be Captai
García-Ramirez and his men, the *federales* they ha
met shortly after their last run-in with the warlord
and Scrawny almost a week ago.

"As it turned out, you could use our help," he said
and then went on to explain that it was he and his me
who had shot the second row of gunmen out of thei
saddles while Chance, Dallas, and Ike had held thei
own.

"Looks like we owe you a debt of gratitude, Cap
tain," Dallas, who had only suffered a minor fles
wound, said.

"Based on the direction you are heading, I assum
your business in Mexico is completed?"

"That's a fact."

"Then your leaving our fair country will be th
answer to my prayers," the captain said with a smil
"Please take care of your friends and leave thes
vermin to me."

Dallas thanked him, then turned to Chance, wh
had lost his strength and plunked himself down on th

ground next to Ike Hadley. Chance pulled out his neckerchief and wiped it across his nose, as though he had the sniffles.

"It's a damn shame, it is," he said softly.

"What's that?"

"Ike ain't never gonna get to see Maria again."

"No, Chance, I reckon he won't," Dallas agreed in a sad tone.

CHAPTER

★ 25 ★

Dallas spent the rest of the afternoon digging t bullet out of Chance's leg and patching him u Chance used cuss words Dallas hadn't heard in son years as the old mountain man cut and dug at the le finally extracting the lead slug.

"Now ain't that a jim dandy?" Dallas said as held the piece of lead up for examination. They bo knew it was only another .44 slug. But then, a piece lead looks a whole lot bigger when it's been dug out your body than it does when you're loading it in your rifle or six-gun.

"Long as it's out, I don't care what you call it," w all Chance had to say about the matter.

But Chance's cussing that afternoon was nothi compared to what he let out when Dallas slapped t ire-red blade of a bowie knife on the wound to cauterize it. Good Lord, Dallas thought to himself when he heard Chance yell, they'll hear him all the way back in Twin Rifles. He silently hoped there were no more gangs like the one they had just encountered n the territory. Like Chance, Dallas had always loved good fight, but at the moment he'd had his fill for the lay.

Captain García-Ramirez did as he said he would, nd he and his men spent the better part of the fternoon stripping the dead *bandidos* of their weapns and tying them over their saddles. The good aptain would have left them there to be picked to the ones by the vultures, but he thought he had seen ome of these faces on wanted posters his own country ad put up. With that in mind, he had ordered his ttle group to secure the bodies to their horses and repare to take them back to headquarters. If there ere indeed a wanted man or two among the lot, he new that his commander would be grateful and pass n that gratitude to him and his men. When the aptain and his men were through, they made a fire parate from that of Dallas and Chance, determined protect the visitors to Mexico until they could ave.

Strong as he was, Chance Carston had passed out ter Dallas had laid that fiery knife on his wounded g. When he came to it was close to sunset and Dallas as holding a plate of beans over the fire to keep them arm.

"'Bout time you come around, boy," the old mounin man said in his most crotchety tone. "I was about toss this to the wolves."

Too weak to argue, Chance took the plate in silence d ate what passed for supper that night. It was the

coffee that seemed to give him strength, he thought
All the beans did was make him break wind.

"What did you do with Ike?" he asked when he wa
through eating.

"Draped him across his saddle," Dallas said, hi
voice turning abruptly sad. "He'll be ready to go whe
you are." After a brief pause, he added, "Kinda late t
be calling the lad by his first name, don't you think?

This time Chance was at a loss for words. "Yeah,
reckon you're right."

"I wouldn't go pondering this affair too awful lon
son," Dallas said after a good deal of silence passe
between them. "As I recall, you got you other things t
think on."

"Such as?"

"Why, that Ferris girl back in Twin Rifles, of cours
The whole town's a-wondering who's gonna propos
first, you or her. Of course, I figger you're gonna do th
gentlemanly thing and ask the woman. Shoot, I migh
even win the bet ary you was to ask her sometime thi
month," Dallas said in a long-drawn-out manne
wanting to make sure Chance knew exactly what h
was talking about.

"You're joshing me, right?"

Dallas was taken aback. Cocking a daring eyebro
at the wounded man, he said, "Not hardly!"

"Is that what keeps you from cadging drinks over t
Ernie Johnson's Saloon?" Chance asked. "Your be
ting money is what pays for your drinks?"

The old-timer's facial expression changed to th
humble one of a man who has been found out. "Trut
of the matter is, yes. Ain't nothing wrong with makir
a little side bet once in a while."

As fitful as his sleep occasionally was that nigh

Chance dreamed of Rachel. He dreamed of meeting her right on the streets of Twin Rifles, but then his dream would run into a difficulty, for he would never know what to say to her. Hell, he had never known what to say to her, what to say to any woman he'd cared a great deal about. Give him a weapon of any sort and Chance Carston could do wonders with it. But ask him to tell a woman what he was feeling about her and he froze up as hard as ice in winter. He was still wondering what he'd say to Rachel when he heard Dallas moving about camp.

Breakfast was considerably better than the evening meal had been. Once again eaten in silence, it consisted of a couple of thick slabs of bacon and a hardtack biscuit each to sop up the grease with. Two cups of coffee hid the fact that bacon and hardtack wasn't an awful lot for breakfast. On the other hand, things could have been worse, and he could remember many a day he'd spent in the war without even a cold cup of coffee to drink.

"Well, don't just sit there, Dallas," Chance said when he was through finishing his coffee. "Let's saddle up."

The mountain man wrinkled his forehead in surprise. "You feel up to it, do you? Hell, you was looking kinda feverish earlier this morning."

Chance often thought Dallas was almost as observant as he was and in this case he was right. The ex-Ranger and cavalryman had indeed felt kind of frenzied when he'd woke up this morning. In fact, if he had his way, he'd likely sleep until noon. But even if he didn't know what to say to her, he still wanted to get back to Rachel Ferris as soon as he could. He also wanted to get back to Twin Rifles so he could see Doc

Riley on a professional basis. This wasn't the firs time he'd been shot in the leg and he didn't want t die of gangrene.

"Fever or not, we might as well get back to town a soon as we can or they'll never be able to bury Ik Hadley in a proper laid-out position," Chance said t hide his real reasons for returning to town wit dispatch.

"Yeah, I reckon being buried doubled over like tha will play havoc on a man's back," Dallas commente as he got up, "although I can't for the life of me se how or why it would matter."

Even in fever and a good bit of pain, Chance wa able to smile at the old mountain man's remark. Dea men seldom had much to say about what went o around them.

They broke camp about the same time as Captai García-Ramirez and his crew of men, both Chanc and Dallas thanking the *federales* profusely for com ing to their aid the day before.

Dallas knew his riding partner didn't get as far as h wanted to that day, but he rode with Chance as far an as hard as the wounded man could stand it. Whic turned out to be the middle of the afternoon that da Actually, it was Dallas who brought them to a halt.

"We'd better make camp over to that water hol Chance," he said with what he hoped Chance woul take to be a fatigued voice. Better that the lad thir some broken-down old man couldn't make it as far a young man with a wound like his, Dallas though Wounded though he might be, a man like Chance sti had a certain amount of pride. That much Dalla knew.

When Chance started to bellyache about the bea being made for supper again, Dallas said, "Don vorry, son. The way I figure it, we oughtta make Twin Rifles in time to get a late breakfast or an early lunch neal from Miss Margaret's table. Tomorrow morning, ve'll just make us a quick pot of coffee, gulp it down, nd make like the devil for town. How's that suit 'ou?"

Dallas knew that Chance was in extreme pain by he grimace on his face and the way he had been riding ll afternoon, but the suggestion the old mountain nan made seemed to perk up his spirits quite a bit. Sets fine with me, as long as this leg of mine don't fall ff first."

The old-timer treated the leg again that night, eeing that it had begun to fester some around the dges. He got out a dark pint-sized bottle he carried in is saddlebags and carefully poured a slosh of Taos ightning on the wound. He then gave Chance a good ng pull on the bottle's contents and took one him-elf. In the back of his mind he told himself that they ad better make Twin Rifles tomorrow or Chance ould be in a lot of trouble, as far as his leg was oncerned.

Dallas had been right about the distance. They ose early the next morning, built a fire, drank their ffee in the dark that precedes dawn, and were in the ddle and riding hard when first light came over the stern horizon.

Perhaps "riding hard" wasn't quite the right term to e. Like the previous morning, Dallas had set a pace thought Chance could follow without putting too uch strain or pain on the wounded man's leg. After , Dallas had been wounded in the lower extremities fore and knew well the kind of pain such a wound uld put a man through. Especially if he was as sperate as Chance Carston seemed to be to get to

the woman he loved. They also had the horse carryin
Ike's body to consider.

When they rode into town Dallas let Chance lea
the way, figuring he'd likely head for the Ferris Hous
and Rachel. But he didn't. Chance walked his hors
into town a block or two before pulling his reins in to
hitching rail about half a block from Doc Riley'
office. Dallas didn't know if the man was deliriou
from the fever and pain or if he'd changed his min
and decided to visit the doctor before looking u
Rachel. Either way, the curiosity of the whole matt
had caught the old mountain man's fancy and h
watched to see what Chance had in mind.

Chance took his time getting off his horse, holdin
on to the cantle of his saddle real sturdylike as he s
his wounded leg on the ground and got his footin
Dallas wasn't sure if it was the pain the wounded ma
felt from dismounting or what that put a mean loo
on Chance's face, but it was the meanest look he'
seen on the man since they'd headed for Monro
Marcus's camp. Chance then reached across the sa
dle and yanked his Spencer rifle from its scabbard.

He was up on the boardwalk, using the Spencer fo
a cane to assist him in his walking, when Rachel cam
running down the street. One of the young lads i
town had seen Dallas and Chance as they slowly ro
back in and had run pell-mell for the Ferris Hous
He'd likely seen the patch-up job Dallas had done o
Chance's leg and relayed it to Rachel, for the woma
had a distraught look about her as she rushed up t
her man.

"Chance, you're hurt! What happened to you?" sh
blurted out. But her words had little effect, for Chan
Carston was a man on a mission.

"Not now, woman," was all he said in reply as h

ept slowly walking toward Doc Riley's office, his eyes traight ahead. Rachel could only stand there in mazement and watch him go. Dallas followed him.

Chance let out a sigh of relief when he saw Wilson Iadley round the corner, apparently just having come own the stairs from the doctor's office for one reason r another. It was as though the man's being there had aved Chance the bother of having to look any further or him.

It was then Dallas thought he knew what was about take place. He carried his Henry rifle in the crook of is arm, his hand firmly agrasp of the stock and lever ction, ready for any trouble Chance might not be ble to handle. But Dallas knew that somehow hance had the situation well in hand.

"Howdy, Chance," Wilson said when he saw hance heading his way. "Say, I been meaning to ask ou if you've seen—"

He never did finish what he had to say, although hance knew good and well he was asking if he'd seen s little brother.

"Hold this!" Chance said, and tossed his Spencer to 'ilson, who caught it in his hand, not six feet from hance. Even without the crutch Chance managed to ep on walking toward Wilson Hadley. Catching the le in a sudden manner like that had thrown the man f guard, and it was all Chance needed. Before ilson knew what was happening, Chance had gotten ose enough to hit him on the jaw as hard as he'd ever t any man. Wilson stumbled backward and before fell to the boardwalk Chance had grabbed the encer out of his hand.

"What the hell are you—"

Wilson, as much a fighter as any of the Hadley others, was about to scramble to his feet when

Chance knocked his arms out from under him, forcin
him back down on the boardwalk. He'd hobbled ove
beside the fallen man and looked down at him now,
good deal of hatred in his eyes.

"You stupid son of a bitch," he hissed at a stunne
Wilson Hadley.

"Now, listen—"

"No, you listen, Wilson Hadley," Chance growle
every bit of mean he could muster now in his voic
"You done everything you could to let Ike know h
wasn't needed around you and Carny. I don't kno
how you done it, but you did. Drove him away so
he'd have to prove himself to . . . himself.

"Runs away from you and winds up with me, of a
people! Ain't that the pot calling the kettle blac
Spent every goddamn waking hour he was with m
trying to prove to me he was tougher than you an
Carny combined. And he did just that. And he died
lot braver and fighting a lot harder than you or I ev
will," Chance said, his voice much calmer than whe
he had started talking. He couldn't believe he'd sa
what he just did; it simply wasn't his way.

"He's dead?" Wilson asked incredulously, his ey
wide open, his mouth agape.

Chance looked over his shoulder at Ike, drape
lifelessly over the saddle of his horse. When h
glanced back at Wilson, he knew the man was in sho
at seeing his brother dead. "I don't know why you d
it, Wilson, but running Ike off was the worst thi
you've ever done."

As though in a trance, Wilson walked over to t
horse and lifted his brother's head to make sure
really was Ike Hadley Chance was talking about.

"Now, woman. Now," Chance said, and Rache
who'd finally followed him down the boardwa

rushed to his side and gave him a hug. Then, silently, she picked up his rifle and positioned herself by his side and helped him climb the stairs to Adam Riley's office.

"Was you there with him, Dallas?" Wilson asked he old mountain man as he stared at the lifeless body of his brother. "Is what he said about Ike true?"

"Every word of it, Wilson. And I can guarantee you one thing for sure. You won't find no bullets in that boy's back. He didn't run from nothing the whole ime he was with us out there." Dallas wasn't about to ell Wilson Hadley what his brother's shortcomings were. And even if he had the desire—which he idn't—this wasn't the time or the place for such a iscussion. "I'll take him over to the undertaker's for ou, if you like."

"Thanks, Dallas. I appreciate it."

But when Dallas was gone down the street, the nger began to fill in Wilson Hadley. It wasn't the first me he'd gotten into a good fight with Chance arston, and it wasn't the first time he'd been bested y the older Carston son. But, damn it, he'd about had nough! Old Will Carston might be Chance's pa and l, but he was still the law and he was more than onest when it came to upholding it in Twin Rifles. By od, it was time to see if the law around here couldn't ork in his favor for once.

Wilson Hadley straightened his hat and headed for ill Carston's office.

CHAPTER ★ 26 ★

Joshua Holly didn't see Dallas and Chance ride int
town that morning. Not that he wouldn't have notice
had he been looking out the window. It was just th
he'd been up all night keeping an eye on the Wa
brothers and was spending most of his time trying
keep awake as he waited for Will Carston to relie
him. The town marshal usually relieved him after he'
had his breakfast over at the Ferris House, and th
morning was no different from the rest. It was just th
Will was a mite late. Oh, well, only a few mo
minutes, Joshua thought to himself as he once aga
glanced at his pocket watch.

"Well, it's about time," he said when Will Carst
walked through the door, a satisfied smile on his fac
"Not only am I tired, but my stomach's been telli

ne it's been without food for the past two hours iow."

"I reckon that's my fault, Joshua," Will said, still ovial in his mood. "Or maybe I should say it's Margaret's fault. Why, she can—"

"Talk. And don't I know. That woman would talk he ear off a Missouri mule, whether it was a-listening r not," Joshua said with a shake of the head.

"I thought you was tired and hungry."

"Oh, I am, Will. I'm just a-saying—"

"Well, I can't do nothing about the tired. But I did ell Margaret to save you a stack of flapjacks and a ness of grits, a slab of ham, and maybe some eggs on ie side," Will said, his smile growing into a tease nore than anything else. "And she said she'd try and ave you some, Joshua, but you know how Margaret is hen it's first come, first served."

The prospect of losing out on the eating of a plate of e food Will had just rattled off was downright isrespectful to Joshua, who grabbed his hat and ade tracks for the door.

"Everything's still in order, I take it?" Will asked efore his deputy could disappear.

"Yup," Joshua said. "Oh, there is one thing. That nhorn gambler come a-stumbling in last night smell-g like he'd had him a jug of who-hit-john. Couldn't iderstand half of what he was saying, so I led him ick to the cell across from the Wades and let him eep it off. I reckon he sobers up you'll want to turn m loose."

With that Joshua Holly was out the door quick as a bbit, on his way to the Ferris House.

Will had made a fresh pot of coffee and was pouring mself the first cup when the door opened and Harry ers and Sam Bayles entered his office. Although he

hadn't caught them doing anything illegal yet, excep
for that run-in they'd had with the tinhorn, he wa
sure they had the potential to be troublemakers. It wa
just the sort of look these types had, a look he ha
made a study of over the years and come to know wel

"What can I do for you gentlemen?" he asked, sti
in a pleasant mood. Margaret Ferris had indeed dor
a lot of talking to him this morning while he ate, an
the subject was Chance and Rachel and what Marg
ret perceived to be their marriage not too far in th
offing. In no uncertain terms, Margaret made it plai
that she wanted Will to talk to Chance about settlir
down—and getting married to her daughter. Will ha
chuckled at the whole subject matter and Margaret
demands, but had promised her he would talk to th
lad when he got back from his trip. The idea of anyor
forcing Chance—a confirmed bachelor, to hear hi
talk—into the institution of marriage was a laughab
one to Will, and it was this that had made him smi
as he'd entered his office that morning.

"Well, Marshal, we was thinking that we knew son
fellas named Wade up in the Indian Territory," Har
Aker said, scratching his jaw. "Figured we'd stop
and take a gander if you don't mind."

"Yeah, might be cousins of ours. They always w
getting in trouble," Sam Bayles said with a slig
blush. Not that he was putting on at all, for the Wa
brothers were distant cousins to Sam Bayles. And th
had definitely been rabble-rousers in their youth.
fact, the trouble they used to get into was likely wh
had caused Sam Bayles to wind up getting in th
trouble he constantly seemed to be getting into.

"I reckon that can be arranged," Will said.

"I suppose you'll be wanting this." Harry Ak
pulled out his six-gun and twirled it about one fing

ıntil it lay in the palm of his hand, offered to the awman butt first. Will was slowly reaching for it when Aker suddenly twirled the revolver around so it nesled in the palm of his hand and was pointing directly t Will. "Not likely, Marshal," he added with the bit f false confidence a man has when he thinks he's got he edge on a man but isn't quite sure within himself. Get that Remington, Sam."

Sam Bayles relieved Will of his six-gun, tossing it nto the corner of the room. That left Will with othing but half a cup of coffee in his hand.

Sam's next move was to grab the keys to the cells off e peg on the wall, open the door to the cell area, and et the Wade brothers out of there before Harry tried kill the lawman and the whole town was after them.

"Come on, Charlie, Ethan," he said as he wiggled e keys in the cell lock until they caught. "Harry's got e marshal covered up front and the horses are out ont. Come on, hurry up." His words were spoken in articular to Ethan, who was having some trouble ılling his boots on.

"Get that lawman back here and we'll lock him up efore we skedaddle," Charlie ordered Sam. In haste, m and the Wades moved into the marshal's main fice, where Harry Aker still had the drop on Will arston.

"Marshal, where's our guns?" Charlie Wade deanded. He had a mad look about him, an urgency to part as quickly as possible.

"Bottom drawer on the left," Will said, indicating s desk with a nod of the head. "It's locked," he ded, and dug a finger into the pocket of his cowhide st, tossing a small key to the outlaw when he found

Charlie Wade undid the lock and pulled out the gun

belts and six-guns for him and his brother. Onc they'd buckled their gun belts on, Charlie turned t Sam Bayles. "Remember what I said about taking hi back to the cell," he said to Sam, giving Will a sho glance. "Me and Ethan will be out front once we get couple of rifles and some more ammunition."

"Right," Sam said. Motioning Will toward th door, he said, "Watch his back, Harry," and pro ceeded back into the cell area, his gun still drawn.

The Wades began to rummage through the drawe of Will's desk, trying to find more ammunition for th two Henry rifles they had taken from Will's rifle rac

Sam Bayles had been so anxious about getting h cousins out of jail that he hadn't even noticed Jerem ah Younger in the cell directly across from that of th Wades. He had lain there as lethargic as a drunk with hangover would be expected to be. And because of h lack of movement, he hadn't been noticed at all. B as Sam Bayles made his way back into the cell are Jeremiah moved to the front of his cell. And in h hand he held his derringer. It was pointed right at Sa Bayles.

"My good man, I would greatly appreciate it if yo would put away that gun," he said in a calm, eve voice. He was doing his best not to sound scared, b his stomach was churning so badly he thought would throw up any minute. "You didn't think would let you and your friend get away with this, d you?" Although it was a weak one, he gave Sam Bayl a smile.

"This ain't the best time to be no hero, tinhorn Will said in an edgy tone. This wasn't really what had in mind for Jeremiah Younger, not at all. The ta lanky gambler was supposed to use that hideout g

›f his only if an emergency came up. Will was upposed to have had everything in hand when these ellows tried to pull their jailbreak. The trouble was Vill's gun was in the corner in the next room and hese fellows all had the guns. How in the hell was the inhorn's popgun going to keep these two at bay? Will ›und himself wondering.

"That's the damn truth," Sam Bayles said, and egan to turn his gun on Jeremiah, derringer or no erringer.

Jeremiah fired both barrels and before Sam Bayles ould get his gun up and aimed at the gambler, he had vo .41-caliber slugs in his chest and he knew he was ›out to die.

Will Carston had always known that there were eapons all around you. A man naturally felt a lot ore comfortable with a six-gun or a rifle in his grasp, even a bowie knife, but when he didn't, well, it dn't mean that he had no weapons at all. All he had do was look around him. As soon as Jeremiah ılled the triggers on his derringer, Will whirled to his ght, bringing his elbow square into Harry Aker's gun m. The coffee he still held in his cup was no longer e piping-hot liquid he had poured originally, but en the lukewarm stuff he threw in the gunman's face ught the man off guard. His elbow had jarred the n loose from the man's grip and when he had mpleted his turn, Will Carston drove his left hand hard and deep into Harry Aker's gut as he could. ie man was doubling over when he brought his knee into the outlaw's face and broke his nose. Harry er sank to the floor, semiconscious and in a good al of pain.

Will saw that Jeremiah was already reaching for the

keys to his cell, which were within easy reach. "Pic
up that six-gun and keep an eye on this bird," h
ordered Jeremiah.

"Yes, sir."

Then he rushed out the door and into his office t
locate his own handgun. After all, the other tw
outlaws were getting away.

Wilson Hadley was just crossing the street when h
saw the door to Will Carston's office open up and tw
men step out. He didn't know them, but he also kne
they were up to no good. Each had a pair of Henr
rifles tucked under his arm, a box or two of shells i
the other hand.

"Say, what are you gents doing with all them rifles?
he asked, still walking toward them.

It was the wrong question to ask and the wrong tim
to get curious about the Wade brothers and the
actions. They gave one another a quick glance an
dropped the rifles and ammunition, knowing full we
they had been found out.

Charlie Wade must have thought there was nothi
left to do but shoot it out, for he was going for his gu
when Wilson Hadley, who already had his Colt .4
drawn, shot the man through the heart.

Ethan Wade was pulling his gun at the same time h
did an about-face and ran right back into the ma
shal's office. He didn't want any part of a gunfight, f
he simply wasn't a gunfighter. Unfortunately, Wi
Carston didn't know that. All he saw was a man wild
waving his six-gun about when he came running bac
inside. And he recognized that man as Ethan Wade

And shot him through the heart.

"Ugly son of a bitch, ain't he?" Wilson Hadley sa

n a noncommittal manner. He still held his own ix-gun, smoke curling up from the end of the barrel.

Will Carston's blood seemed to boil whenever he aw a Hadley anymore, although he wasn't sure why. 'orce of habit, perhaps. "I suppose you killed the ther one?" he asked in as mean and growly a manner s he could muster.

"Matter of fact, I did," Wilson said. Then, seeing ıe expression on Will's face, he knew he wouldn't get nywhere, no matter how legitimate his complaint. Ie holstered his gun, said, "Aw, hell," and disap-eared as abruptly as he had appeared.

Will must have had an awfully haggard look about im, for when Jeremiah Younger entered the room, he ıid, "I daresay, Marshal, you look like a man who is ıite suddenly old."

Age had always been a touchy subject with Will arston and now wasn't the time to discuss it with m. With the same hard voice he had used on Wilson adley, he turned to the gambler and said, "I ain't *d.* I've just lived a hard life."

As though he didn't care one way or another, remiah Younger handed Will a six-gun and the jail ys. "The one with the bloody nose is in his cell. And von't need the gun for what I have to do."

Then, as if he had never been a part of any of this ɔodshed, Jeremiah Younger left the marshal's office. : too had something that needed taking care of.

CHAPTER
★ 27 ★

Jeremiah found Wilson Hadley down by the live: stable, saddling his horse. He didn't have to see hi back at the jail to know that the man was extreme disappointed. Besides, it was hard not to hear tv distinctly gruff-sounding voices like Will Carston aı Wilson Hadley when they were upset about som thing. And at the moment he was more concern with the plight of Wilson Hadley than he was that Will Carston. The marshal had given the impressi of being a man who was used to being in charge everything he was involved with. But Wilson Hadle well, he had proved to be a rather sensitive man, f all the rudeness he was prone to display. Jeremiah h enjoyed listening to the man and his personal pro lems, enjoyed even more trying to help him fi answers to those problems. Whether the big, rough-looking man knew it or not, he had had a marked effect on him.

"You can't run away from your problems, Wilson," Jeremiah Younger said in that soft tone he had, the one he had practiced so he wouldn't sound preachy. "You know that, don't you?"

"Who says?"

"I say, for one," Jeremiah replied. "And I think you know it, too." When Wilson didn't answer him, he added, "Don't you?"

The gambler had put him in an awkward position, and Wilson Hadley didn't like being put in awkward positions. His initial reaction was to fight back, just like he always did.

"It don't make no difference, tinhorn. It's never made any difference," Wilson said, tightening the cinch on his saddle. It was the first time he'd called Jeremiah a tinhorn since he'd become friendly with the man. It was part of that inborn desire to fight when he was challenged. "Me and my brothers ain't never been much good to this town. Even when I do something right, I can't get no credit for it. Don't mind telling you, I've about had my fill of it." Silently, he walked his horse to the entrance of the livery.

Jeremiah was right behind him, trying his hardest to think of something to say. He took a chance.

"If you ask me, Wilson Hadley, you aren't running away from this town, you're running away from *yourself,*" Jeremiah said in the strongest voice he could muster.

Wilson dropped the reins of his horse and turned around to face Jeremiah. And as he did he formed a fist and swung it hard, striking the gangly gambler square on the jaw and knocking him ass over teakettle.

Jeremiah Younger could only lie there in shock tha
the man he had become so friendly with could do suc
a thing to him. "That was a big mistake, tinhorn,
Wilson growled. "And I was just getting to like you.

Hadley shook his head and mounted his horse a
Jeremiah Younger got back on his feet. Once again th
gambler was trying to come up with the right words t
say to this man. Wilson Hadley was about to leav
when Jeremiah rushed over to the front of the hors
and grabbed the reins.

"Don't you see, Wilson? It doesn't work that wa
You simply can't spend your life complaining abo
the world owing you a living or anything else," he sai
in one last desperate attempt at reason.

"What the hell are you talking about?"

"Wilson, the world owes you absolutely *nothin*
You see, my good man, it's been here longer tha
either of us. What you must do is some good in th
world. Then and only then will it be returned to you i
kind."

"And how the hell am I supposed to do that?" Th
longer the gambler kept him here, the angrier Wilso
Hadley became.

"Why, you've already done it, Wilson! Today. Th
morning. You stopped a treacherous outlaw fro
escaping jail," Jeremiah said, a bit of excitement i
his voice now. "Don't you see? It's a start."

"All right, pilgrim, say it is," Wilson concede
"Where do I go from there? What do I do?"

The words were coming now and, just as ha
happened before in this town, whenever he'd bee
asked to come up with a solution to a person
problem, he had spoken the right words. He didr
know how they came to him, they just did. And
amazed him as much as it did those he spoke to.

"On a personal note, you could start by helping me, Vilson," he said in a deadly serious tone.

"Help you?" Wilson said incredulously. "What ind of help could you want?"

There was a certain sadness in Jeremiah's disposiion now, and it was one Wilson Hadley hadn't onfronted before. "I forgot. You weren't there." eremiah reached in his pocket and pulled out the erringer, which was now empty. "I'm afraid I killed ne of those outlaws this morning, too. I've never illed a man before, did you know that? Never. How o you cope with it, Wilson? It doesn't seem to bother ou. But me—I've a very queasy feeling in my omach at the moment." It was no act he was putting n, nothing he was saying just for the benefit of ilson Hadley.

"It's something, all right, taking the most important ing a man has," Wilson said with a shake of the ead, knowing full well what the man before him was lking about. "But as long as you was doing right, I ckon you got nothing to worry about. Never did give much thought until you brought it up."

"Does any of what I've said make any sense, ilson?" Jeremiah asked. "Can you see—"

"I need to do some thinking, Jeremiah," Wilson id, and urged his horse forward.

"Don't be long, Wilson."

Wilson Hadley stopped and looked back over his oulder, a curious frown about him. "Why do you that?"

"Just don't be long," was all Jeremiah Younger uld say.

Then Wilson Hadley rode out of town.

CHAPTER

★ 28 ★

Well, Marshal, I guess I'll be leaving your fair com
munity," Jeremiah said as he rode up to Will Carsto
who was now giving orders to the town undertaker o
the disposition of the three bodies. "I hope th
information I passed on to you was of use."

"Oh, it was, Jeremiah," Will said. "I just didn
figure on you taking on the role of a hero and all."

"Believe me, sir, I'm not a hero by any means," h
said with a weak smile. He never had been able to ta
compliments all that well. "I assure you, my actio
were simply those of a desperate man."

"I don't know, Jeremiah, I wouldn't go countin
myself out like that," Will said. "It took a lot of guts
stand up to any one of those yahoos. Even with th
popgun of yours."

Jeremiah Younger had saddled his own horse after Vilson Hadley rode off. He had then made a short top at the Ferris House and, without anyone being he wiser, checked out of his room, leaving the money or his bill at the check-in counter. Perhaps that was vhy Margaret Ferris had followed him down to the narshal's office.

"You're not leaving, are you? You *can't* leave," she aid emphatically as she reached Will's side. "Why, nere's room for you in this town. Twin Rifles *needs* ou."

Jeremiah shrugged, his smile growing even more neepish, if that were possible. "But what could I ossibly offer you fine people? I'm certainly no great nakes as a gambler. And I believe even Carny Hadley getting tired of seeing my face."

"Did it ever cross your mind, Jeremiah, that maybe ou've missed your calling?" Margaret asked.

"Missed my calling? Why, my good woman, what ould you possibly be talking about?" The would-be ambler appeared to be thoroughly confused now.

"When I first met you, Jeremiah, you gave off the npression of a man who was wandering about, not re where he was going or what he wanted to do," argaret said. "I thought giving you a job to do, rrying meals over to Carny Hadley, would give you sense of accomplishment. But it seems that in the ort time you've been here, why, you've helped out ore than me or Carny Hadley or Will. Why, Betty athaway was saying the other day how she appreci-ed your advice on getting along in life, now that e's a widow."

"Please, it was nothing, a mere slip of the tongue," emiah said, a streak of red creeping up the back of neck.

'I don't think so, friend," Will said. "Tom Rainey

was telling me the other day how you talked to hin and the missus after she lost that child. Now, that' more than I could ever do in a situation like that. Nc sir. Takes a special knack to do that kind of thing."

"Please, Marshal, I couldn't," the tall man said, a though begging off the responsibility that was bein thrown his way.

"Well, you'd better." Over his shoulder Jeremia saw Wilson Hadley walking his horse toward then The tone of his voice was as gruff and hard as ever an Jeremiah knew he meant business. "Let me tell yo folks something. You find you a collar for this ma and you'll have you another crackerjack preacher."

Will glanced at Margaret. "Now there's an idea." T Jeremiah he said, "Know your Bible, do you?"

"Well, yes, I have dipped into the scriptures o more than one occasion." Jeremiah was sudden feeling not only embarrassed but a bit nervous as we "But don't you already have a man of the cloth to ho your church services? I appreciate the offer, th thought, but how could I ever gain the confidence the community?"

"If it's people you're looking for who have faith i you, Jeremiah, I'll be the first," Wilson Hadley sai He didn't seem ashamed or contrary whatsoever whe he said, "I'd like you to speak at Ike's funeral."

"Of course, Wilson," Jeremiah said, a bit of teary-eyed look overcoming him. "I'm sorry to hear it, but I'd be honored."

"I think Ike would be, too," Will said, and everyor knew that he meant what he said. "Fact of the matt is, there's someone around here who's been itching f a well-versed preacher to marry off her daughter Will added with a sly glance toward Margaret.

"Oh, Will, hush now," Margaret said, and pr ceeded to invite Jeremiah down to the Ferris Hou 'or some coffee and pie and perhaps a talk about how vell he would be received in the community.

When they were gone, Will turned his attention to Vilson Hadley. "Wilson, I need to talk to you."

"I can't for the life of me figure out why, unless it vas to warn me to stay out of trouble." The oldest Iadley's tone hadn't softened any once he knew it was he marshal he was talking to.

"You know, you and Carny haven't been all that asy to keep a handle on over the years."

"True."

"But the last year or so, I'd say the two of you have ome around to acting like you really belong in this ommunity."

Wilson shrugged. "We'd like to think so, Carny and ie."

"I don't recall many a time when we said thanks to ou—meaning the people in town and all, you underand," Will said. This time it was he who was feeling tad bit embarrassed.

"That's likely true too."

"Well, it may be mighty late to be doing it, but you ll Carny I said thanks for all the good you two have ne in the last year or so."

Wilson gave Will Carston a quick nod of the head. 'll do that, although there ain't no telling how he'll ke it."

"There's one other thing, Wilson. Thanks for stopng that man this morning. Having you around came right handy."

"Sure, Marshal."

"Come to think of it, don't be surprised ary I come : you to pin on a badge the next time I'm needing a puty," Will said. At first he didn't think he'd be able say it, not at all sure what Wilson Hadley's reaction uld be. But the words came out surprisingly easy.

"I'll keep that in mind, Marshal." Wilson pause a moment before saying, "You won't be sorr Will."

"No, Wilson, I don't think I will either."

Over at Adam Riley's office, Rachel stood by as th doctor finished patching up Chance's leg good an proper. He had cleansed the wound and then applie disinfectant to it before rewrapping it. He had als admonished Chance about the severity of the woun if he had gone any longer without giving it the care deserved.

"Believe me, Doc, Dallas warned me about it all th way across the Rio Grande," Chance said with onl half a grin. "Near got me to believing my leg woul fall off if we didn't speed up our horses and mak tracks on the trail."

"Well, he was right." With a shake of the hea Adam added, "Sometimes that old codger amazes m with what he knows."

"Don't let him hear that. He might take offense."

Adam Riley laughed and said, "I suppose you tw want to be alone for a while." To Rachel he sai "Don't make it too long. He's going to need his rest

When the doctor had left the room, Rachel quick made her way to Chance, who was sitting up in be As best she could in that position, she threw her arm around him and kissed him with a passion.

"Oh, I've missed you, darling," she said when the lips parted. "I've missed you so much."

"Me too," Chance replied. "Fact is, I been thinki about you. About us."

"Oh?"

"Yeah." He took her hand in his and, in a voice soft as he could make it, said, "I ain't never been hat good with words, but what would you think about etting married to me? I know I ain't got much to offer ut the makings of a horse ranch—"

Before he could get out another word, Rachel had ll but crawled up on top of him and began to kiss him ı that same passionate way. Not that Chance tried to op her any. In fact, he was encouraging, if anything.

"Oh, yes! You don't know how long I've waited to ear you say that, darling," she said in a joyous voice.

"I know it will take you a while to make your edding dress and all, but I want you to know I'll wait r you, Rachel," Chance said, still feeling kind of umsy with his words.

Rachel leaned over him again and kissed him, this me a bit gentler than before. Then she sat down next him on the bed, a mischievous smile about her. 'ou silly fool. There won't be any waiting. None at l."

Chance frowned, confused. "Ma'am?"

She ran a smooth hand along the side of his bearded ce. "Honey," she said in a sultry way, "I started aking that wedding dress the day you came back om the war."

Then she leaned over and kissed him again, and ey both knew, deep in their hearts, that everything uld be all right.

Printed in the United States
By Bookmasters